NAME _____

Lesson 1.1
IDENTIFYING 2-D SHAPES

This is a square.

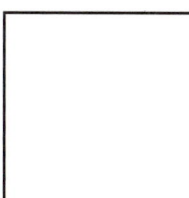

A square has four sides.

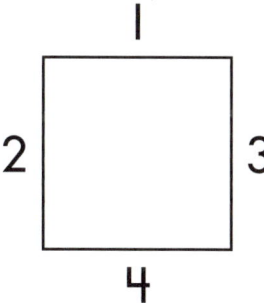

A square has four corners.

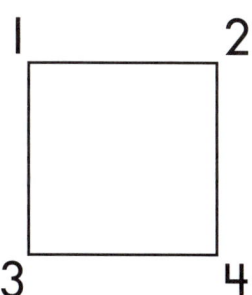

Color the squares.

Spectrum Shapes
Kindergarten

Chapter 1, Lesson 1
Identifying Shapes

5

NAME _____

Lesson 1.1
IDENTIFYING 2-D SHAPES: SQUARES

Circle the squares.

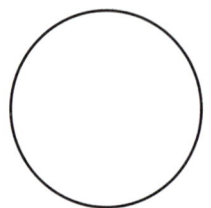  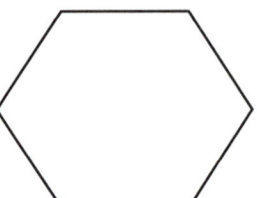 

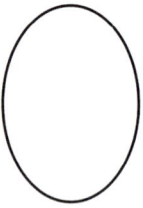   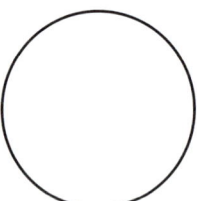

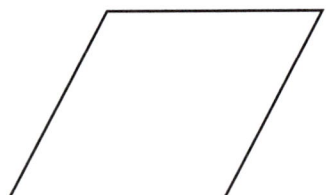 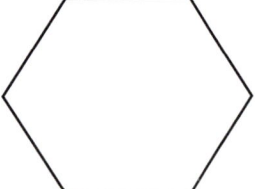  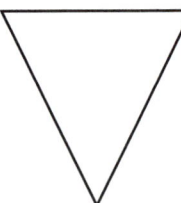

   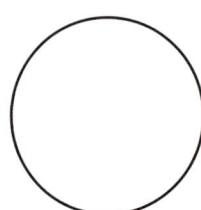

Spectrum Shapes
Kindergarten

Chapter 1, Lesson 1
Identifying Shapes

Shapes

Kindergarten

Published by Spectrum®
an imprint of Carson-Dellosa Publishing
Greensboro, NC

Spectrum®
An imprint of Carson-Dellosa Publishing LLC
P.O. Box 35665
Greensboro, NC 27425 USA

© 2016 Carson-Dellosa Publishing LLC. Except as permitted under the United States Copyright Act, no part of this publication may be reproduced, stored, or distributed in any form or by any means (mechanically, electronically, recording, etc.) without the prior written consent of Carson-Dellosa Publishing LLC. Spectrum® is an imprint of Carson-Dellosa Publishing LLC.

Printed in the USA • All rights reserved.   ISBN 978-1-4838-3104-6

01-053167784

Table of Contents — Shapes

Chapter 1 Identifying Shapes
Lessons 1–22 5–42

Chapter 2 Analyzing and Comparing Shapes
Lessons 1–4 43–50

Chapter 3 Identifying Shapes within Pictures
Lessons 1–13 51–63

Chapter 4 Describing the Orientation of Objects and Shapes
Lessons 1–3 64–69

Chapter 5 Tracing, Drawing, and Composing Shapes
Lessons 1–3 70–77

Shapes Answers 78–96

NAME _____

Lesson 1.2
IDENTIFYING 2-D SHAPES: CIRCLES

This is a circle.

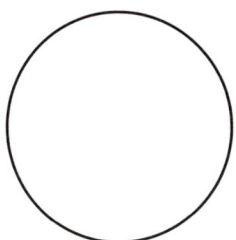

A circle is round.

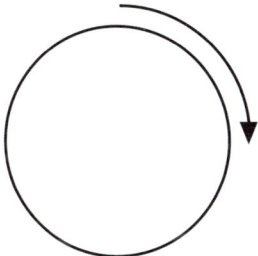

Color the circles.

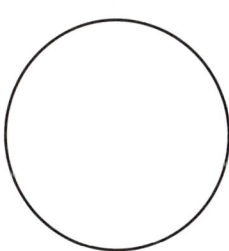  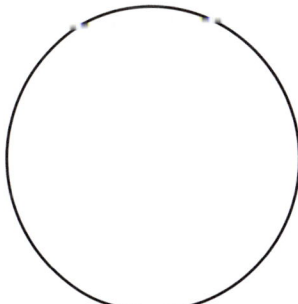

Spectrum Shapes
Kindergarten

Chapter 1, Lesson 2
Identifying Shapes

7

NAME _____

Lesson 1.2
IDENTIFYING 2-D SHAPES: CIRCLES

Put an X over the circles.

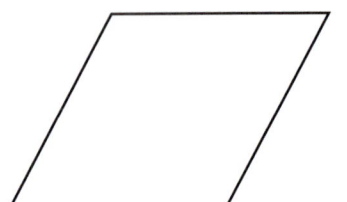 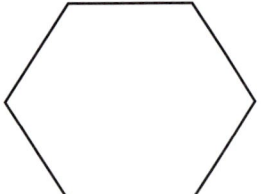 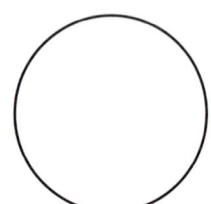 

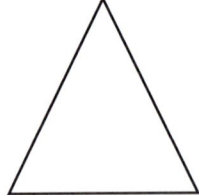 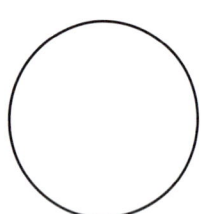  

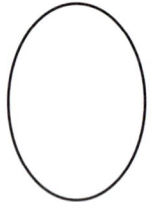 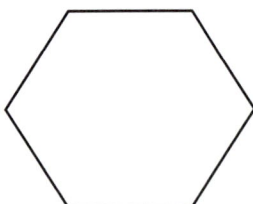  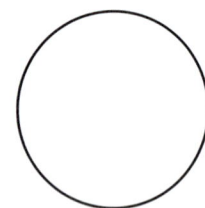

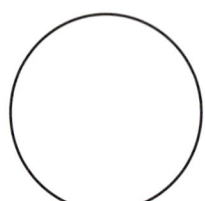   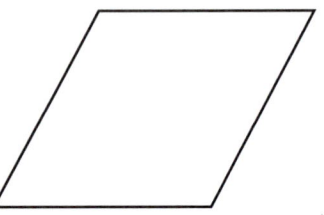

Spectrum Shapes
Kindergarten

Chapter 1, Lesson 2
Identifying Shapes

NAME _____

Lesson 1.3
IDENTIFYING 2-D SHAPES: TRIANGLES

This is a triangle.

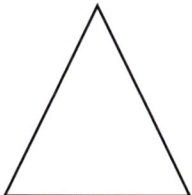

A triangle has three sides.

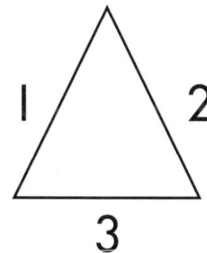

A triangle has three corners.

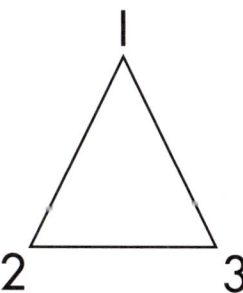

Color the triangles.

 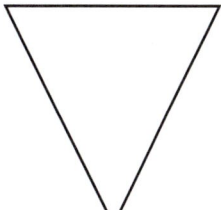 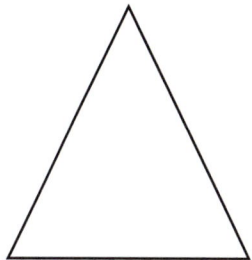

Spectrum Shapes
Kindergarten

Chapter 1, Lesson 3
Identifying Shapes

NAME _____

Lesson 1.3
IDENTIFYING 2-D SHAPES: TRIANGLES

Circle the triangles.

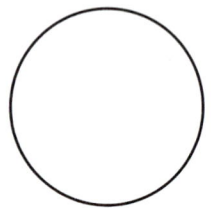  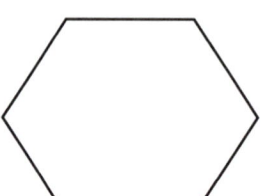 

  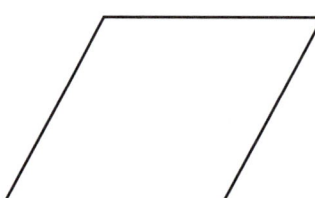 

 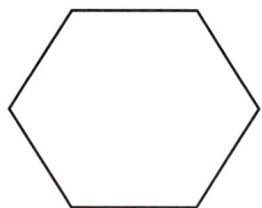  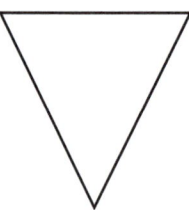

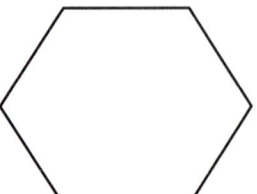  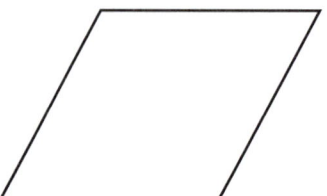 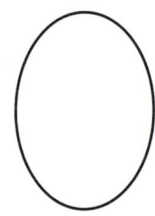

Spectrum Shapes
Kindergarten

Chapter 1, Lesson 3
Identifying Shapes

NAME _____

Lesson 1.4
IDENTIFYING 2-D SHAPES: RECTANGLES

This is a rectangle.

A rectangle has four sides.
Two sides are short.
Two sides are long.

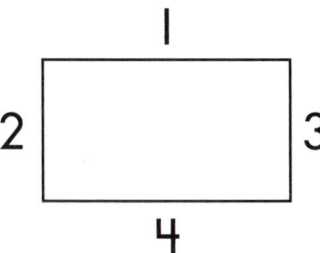

A rectangle has four corners.

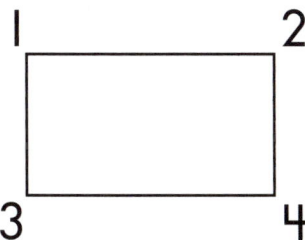

Color the rectangles.

NAME _____

Lesson 1.4
IDENTIFYING 2-D SHAPES: RECTANGLES

Circle the rectangles.

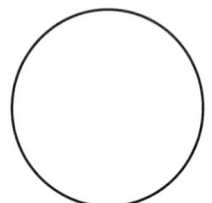  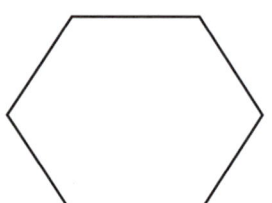 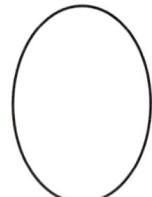

   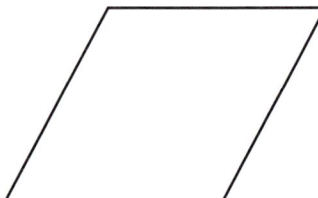

 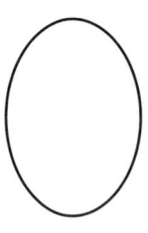  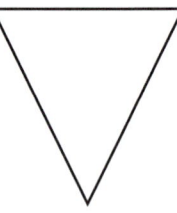

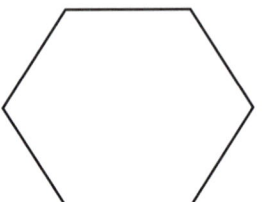 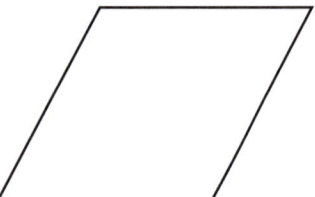  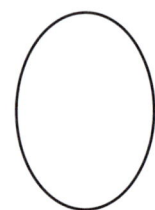

Spectrum Shapes
Kindergarten

Chapter 1, Lesson 4
Identifying Shapes

NAME

Lesson 1.5
IDENTIFYING 2-D SHAPES: OVALS

This is an oval.

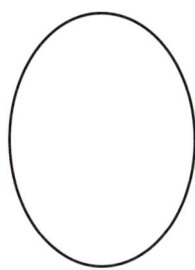

An oval has rounded sides.

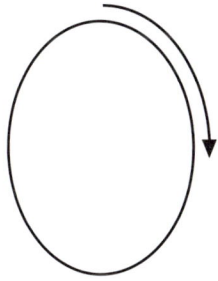

Color the ovals.

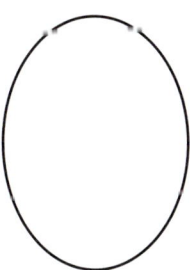 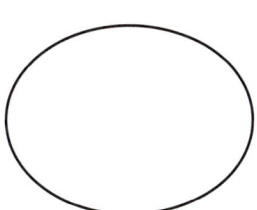 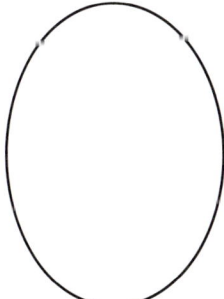

Spectrum Shapes
Kindergarten

Chapter 1, Lesson 5
Identifying Shapes

NAME _____

Lesson 1.5
IDENTIFYING 2-D SHAPES: OVALS

Put an X on the ovals.

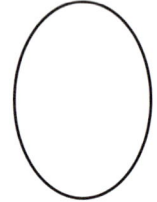  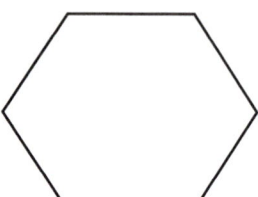 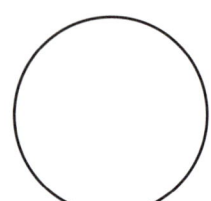

 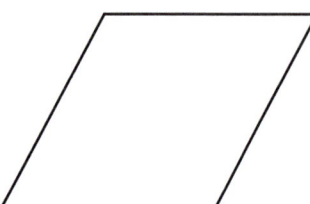  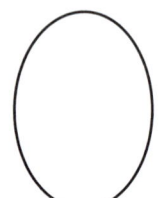

 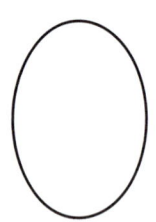  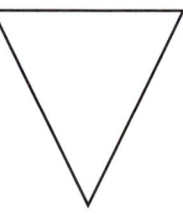

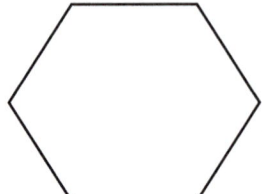 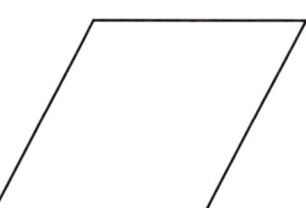  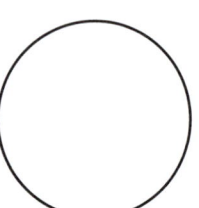

Spectrum Shapes
Kindergarten

Chapter 1, Lesson 5
Identifying Shapes

NAME _____

Lesson 1.6
IDENTIFYING 2-D SHAPES: RHOMBUSES

This is a rhombus.

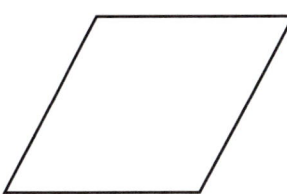

A rhombus has four sides.

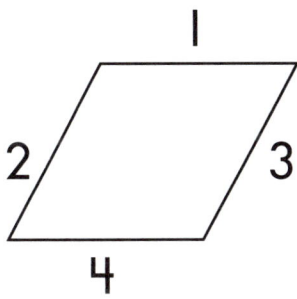

A rhombus has four corners.

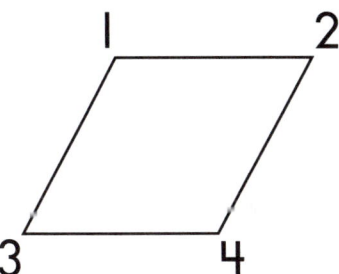

Color the rhombuses.

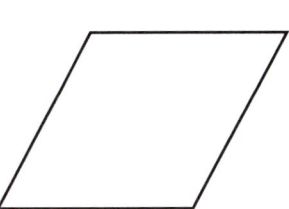 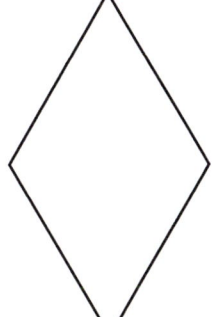 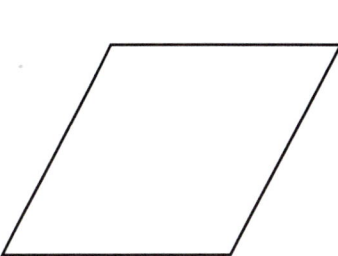

Spectrum Shapes
Kindergarten

Chapter 1, Lesson 6
Identifying Shapes

15

NAME _____

Lesson 1.6
IDENTIFYING 2-D SHAPES: RHOMBUSES

Circle the rhombuses.

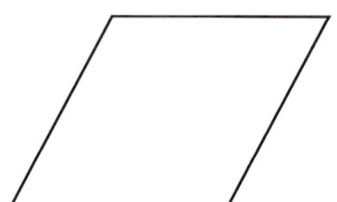  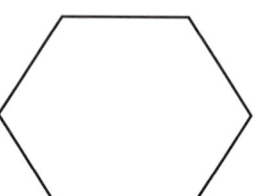 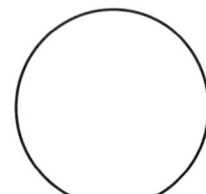

   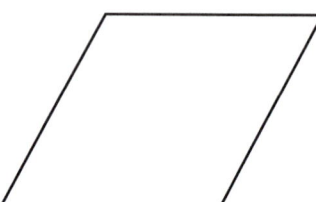

 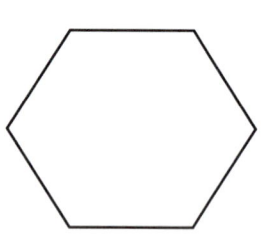 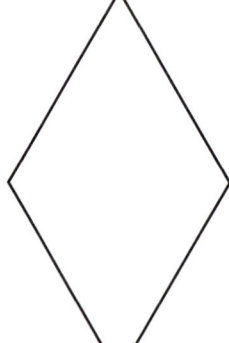 

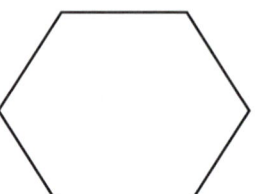 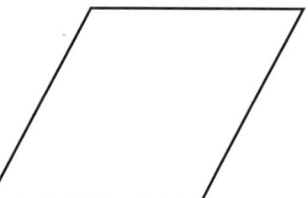  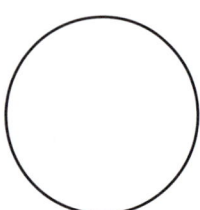

Spectrum Shapes
Kindergarten

Chapter 1, Lesson 6
Identifying Shapes

NAME _____

Lesson 1.7
IDENTIFYING 2-D SHAPES: HEXAGONS

This is a hexagon.

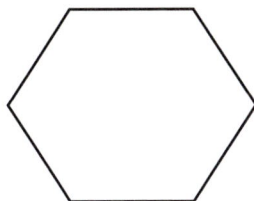

A hexagon has six sides.

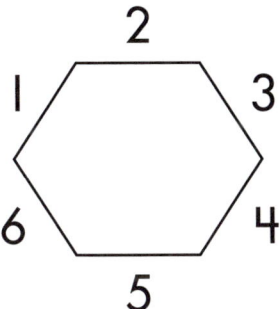

A hexagon has six corners.

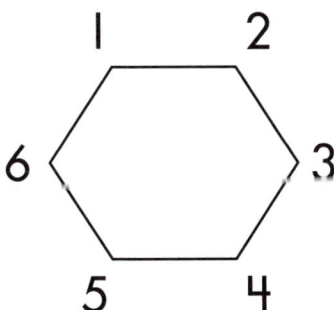

Color the hexagons.

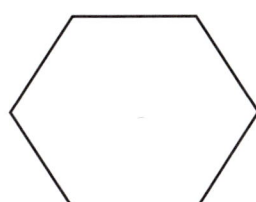 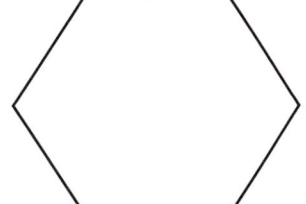 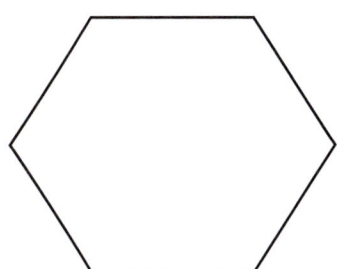

Spectrum Shapes
Kindergarten

Chapter 1, Lesson 7
Identifying Shapes

NAME _____

Lesson 1.7
IDENTIFYING 2-D SHAPES: HEXAGONS

Circle the hexagons.

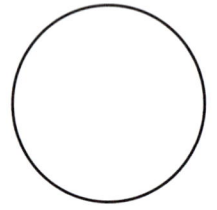  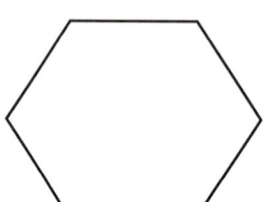 

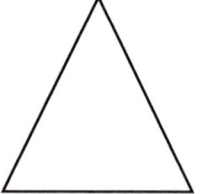   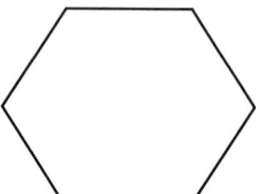

 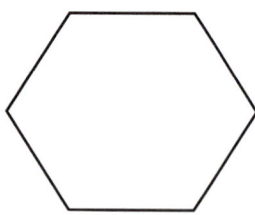 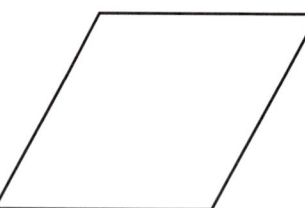 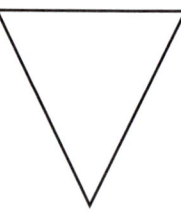

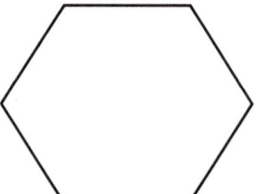 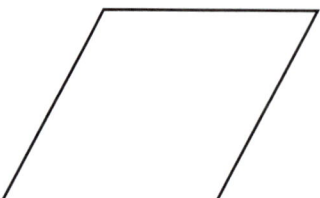  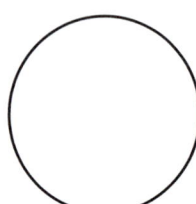

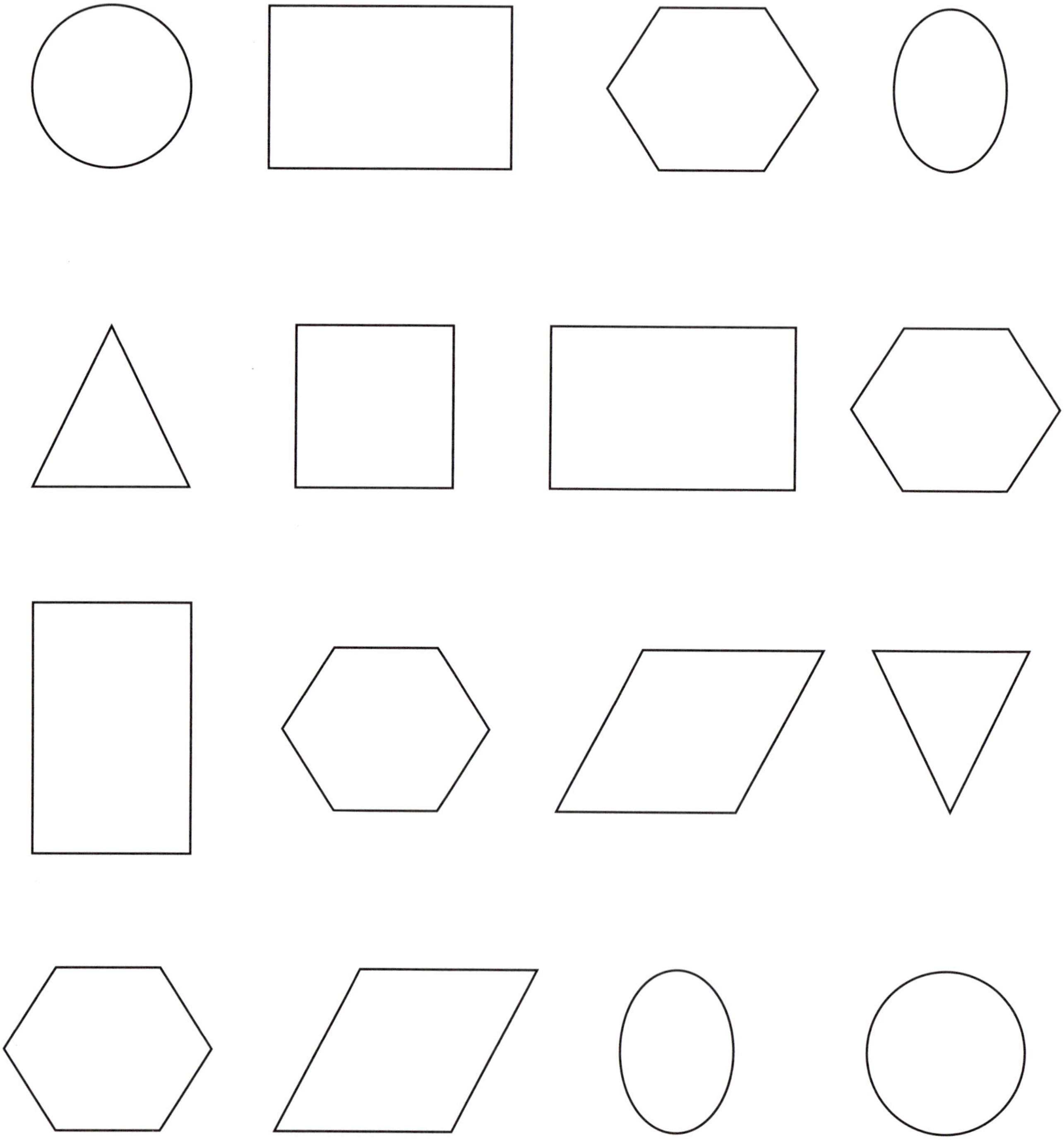

Spectrum Shapes
Kindergarten

Chapter 1, Lesson 7
Identifying Shapes

NAME _____

Lesson 1.8
IDENTIFYING 2-D SHAPES: SAME ORIENTATIONS, SAME SIZES

Color the squares green.

Color the circles red.

Color the triangles blue.

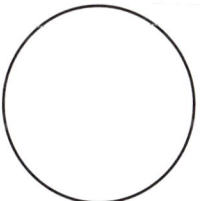 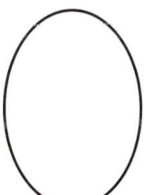 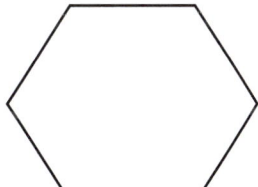 

 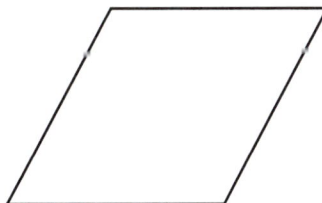  

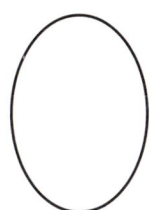 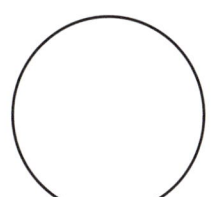  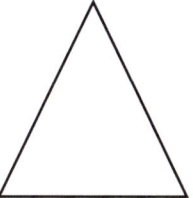

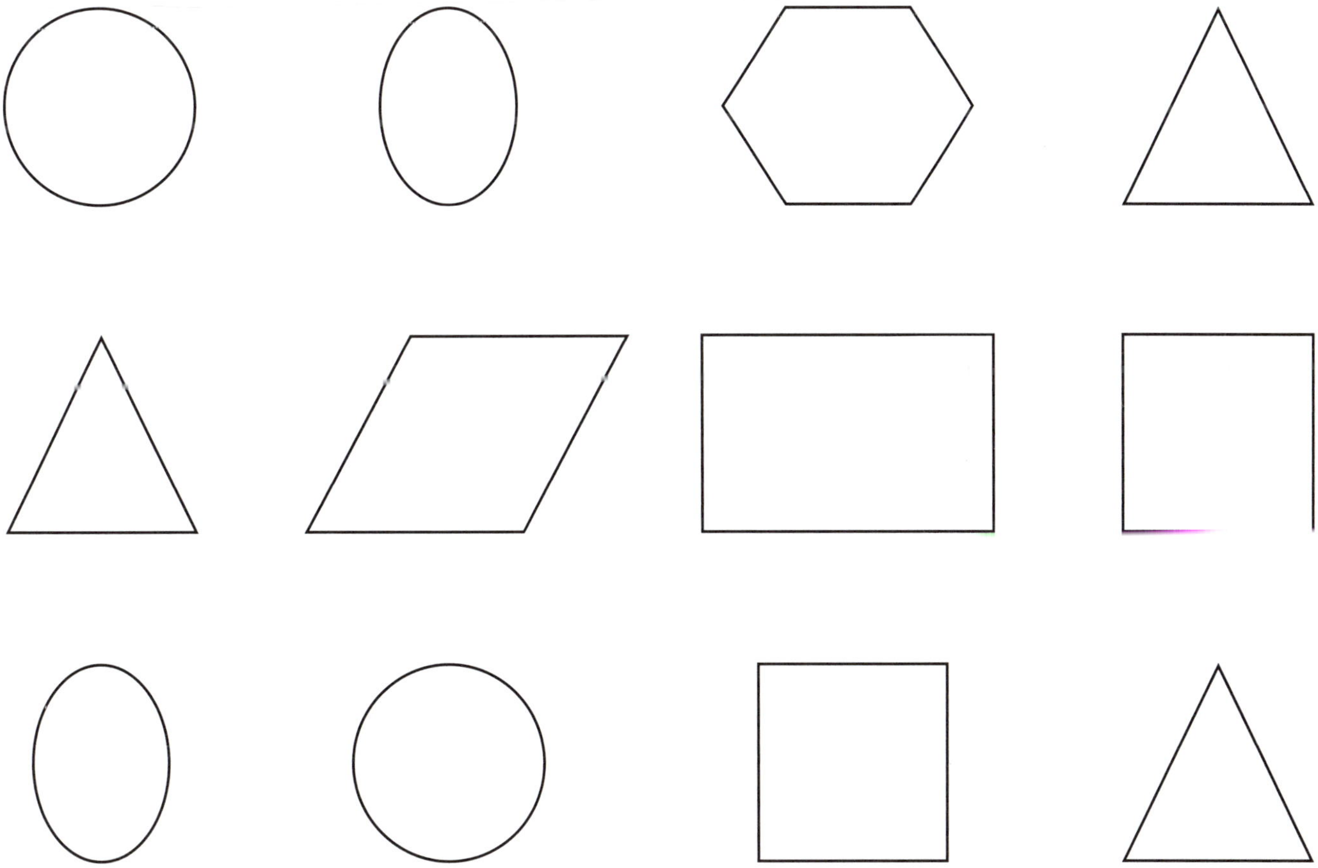

Spectrum Shapes
Kindergarten

Chapter 1, Lesson 8
Identifying Shapes

19

NAME _____

Lesson 1.9
IDENTIFYING 2-D SHAPES: DIFFERENT ORIENTATIONS, SAME SIZES

Color the rectangles yellow.

Color the triangles blue.

Color the ovals purple.

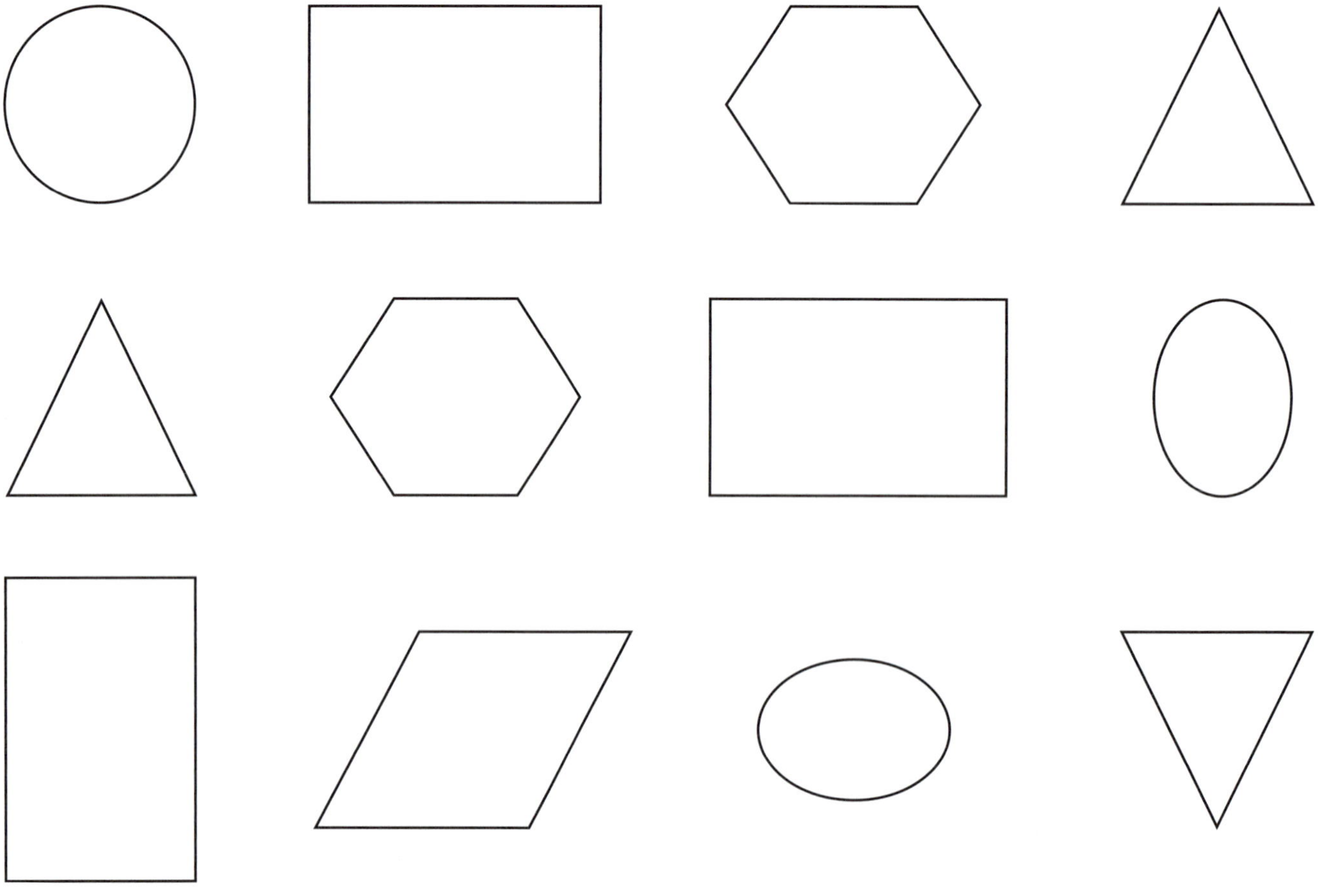

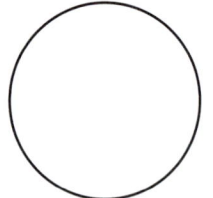  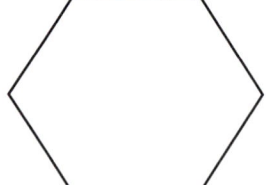 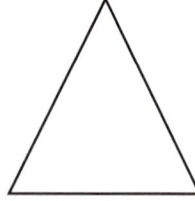

 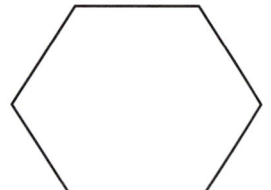  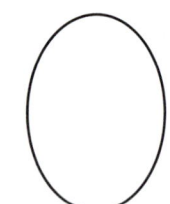

 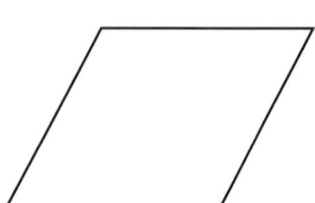 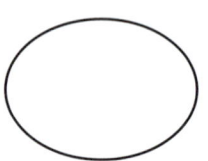 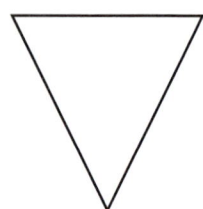

Spectrum Shapes
Kindergarten

Chapter 1, Lesson 9
Identifying Shapes

NAME _____

Lesson 1.10
IDENTIFYING 2-D SHAPES: SAME ORIENTATIONS, DIFFERENT SIZES

Color the rhombuses pink.

Color the circles red.

Color the hexagons orange.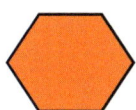

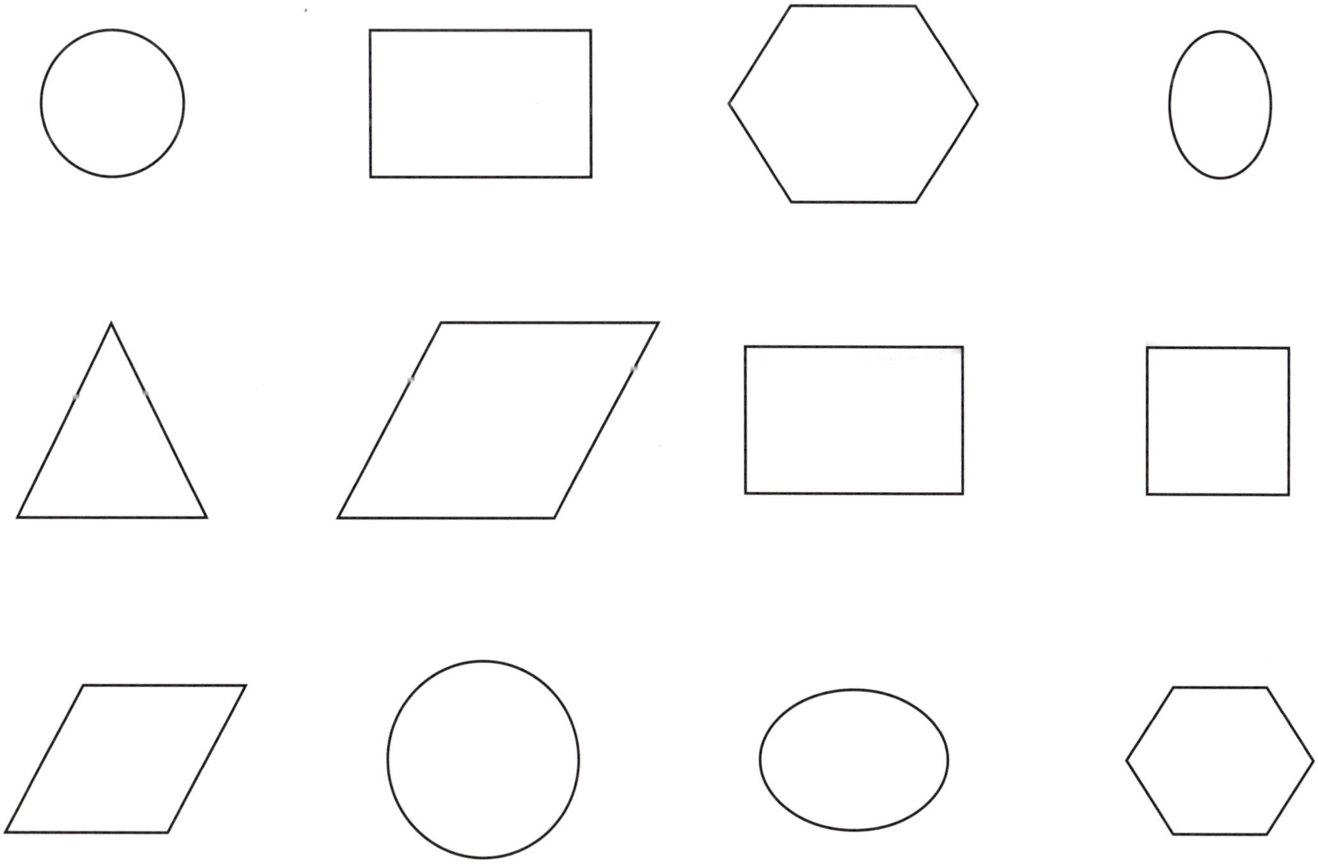

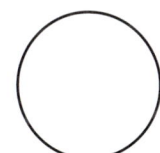  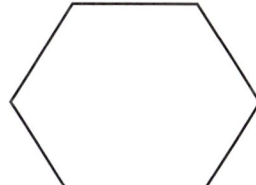 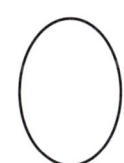

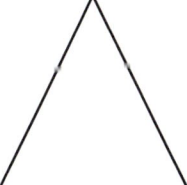 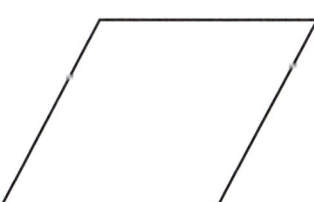  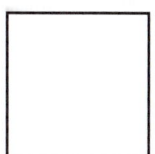

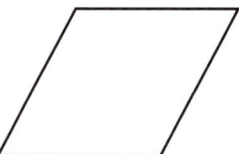 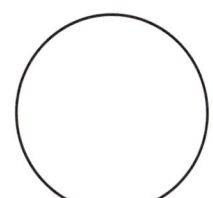 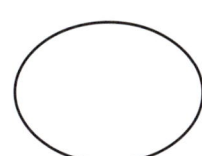 

Spectrum Shapes
Kindergarten

Chapter 1, Lesson 10
Identifying Shapes

NAME _____

Lesson 1.11
IDENTIFYING 2-D SHAPES: DIFFERENT ORIENTATIONS, DIFFERENT SIZES

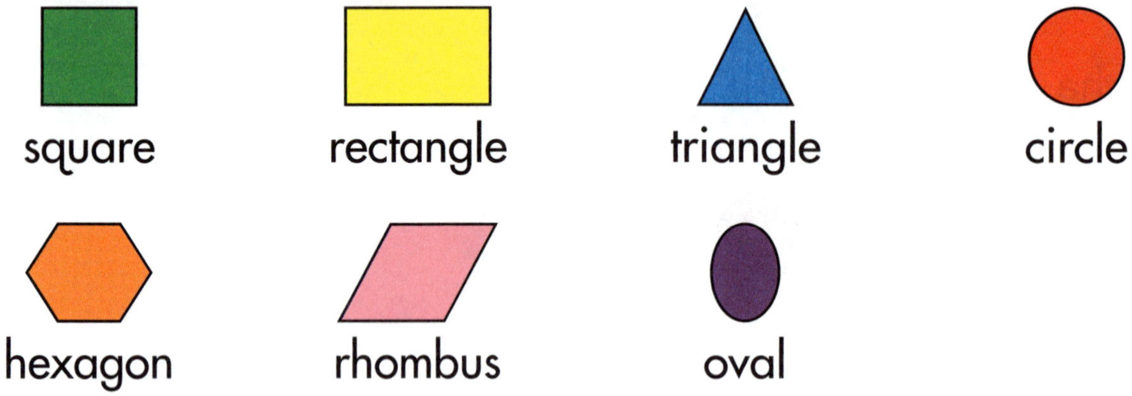

square   rectangle   triangle   circle

hexagon   rhombus   oval

Color the shapes to match the shapes at the top of the page.

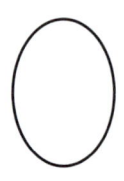  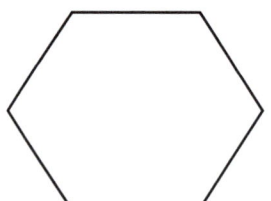 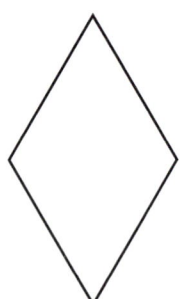

 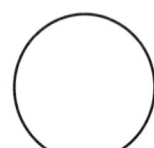  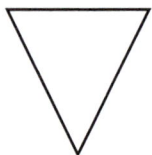

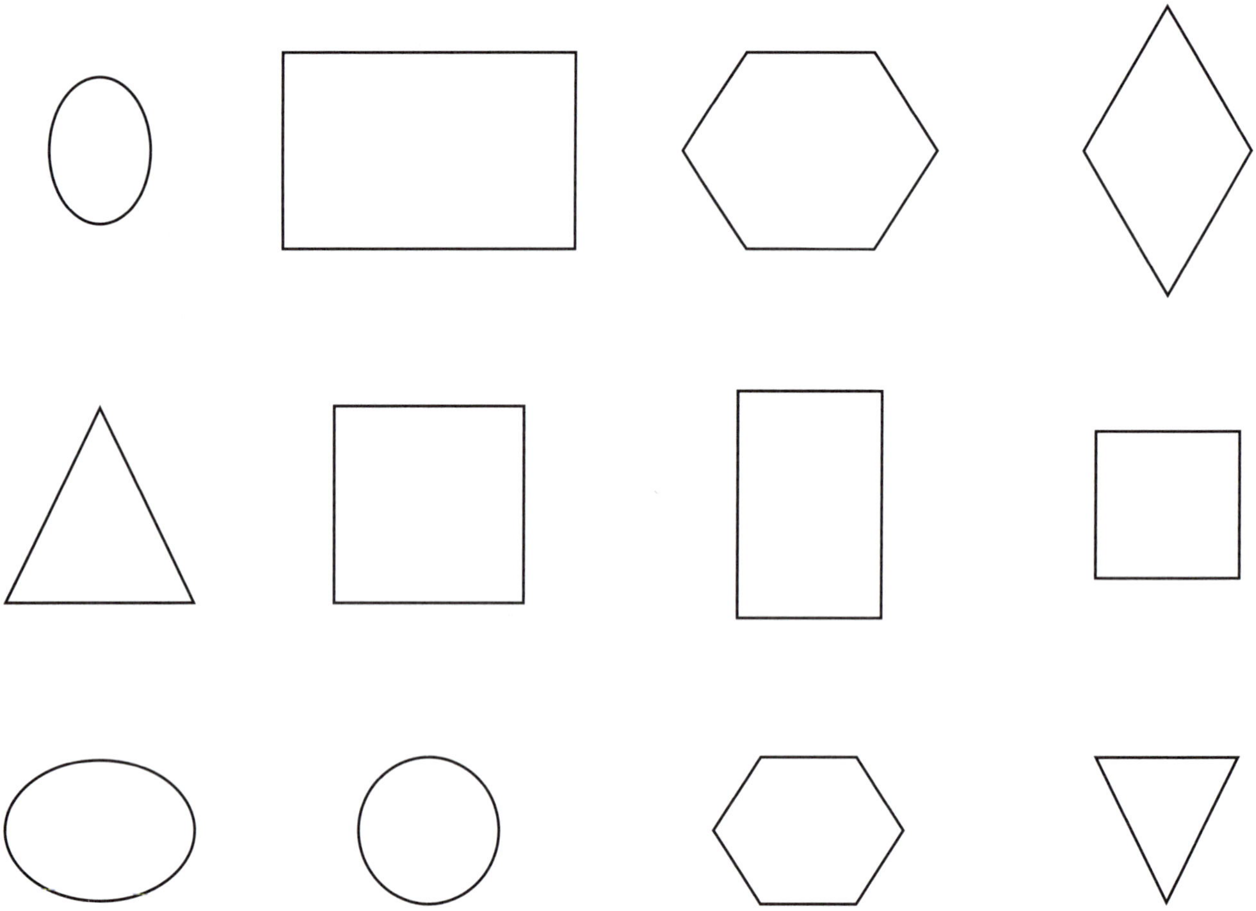

Spectrum Shapes
Kindergarten
22

Chapter 1, Lesson 11
Identifying Shapes

Lesson 1.12
IDENTIFYING 3-D SHAPES: CUBES

This is a cube. It looks like a square box.

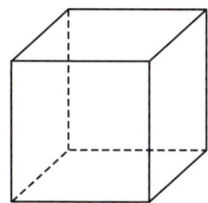

A cube has six flat sides or faces.

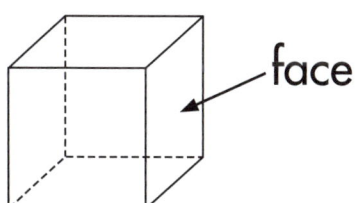

A cube has eight corners or vertices.

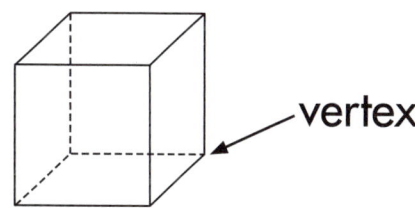

A cube slides and stacks. It does not roll.

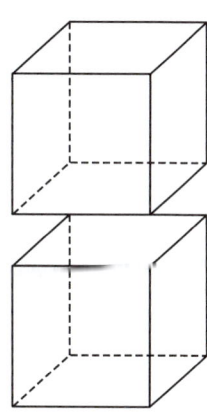
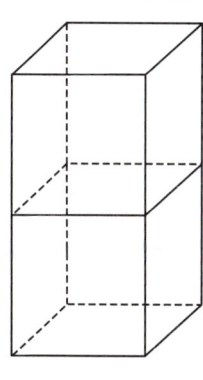

Color the cubes.

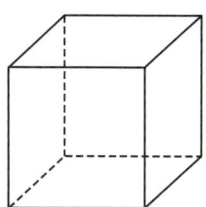
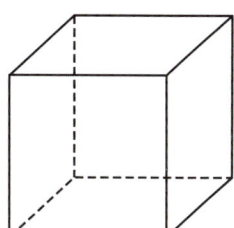
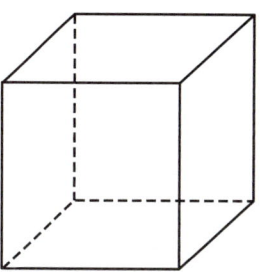

Spectrum Shapes
Kindergarten

Chapter 1, Lesson 12
Identifying Shapes

23

NAME ______________________________

Lesson 1.12

IDENTIFYING 3-D SHAPES: CUBES

Circle the cubes.

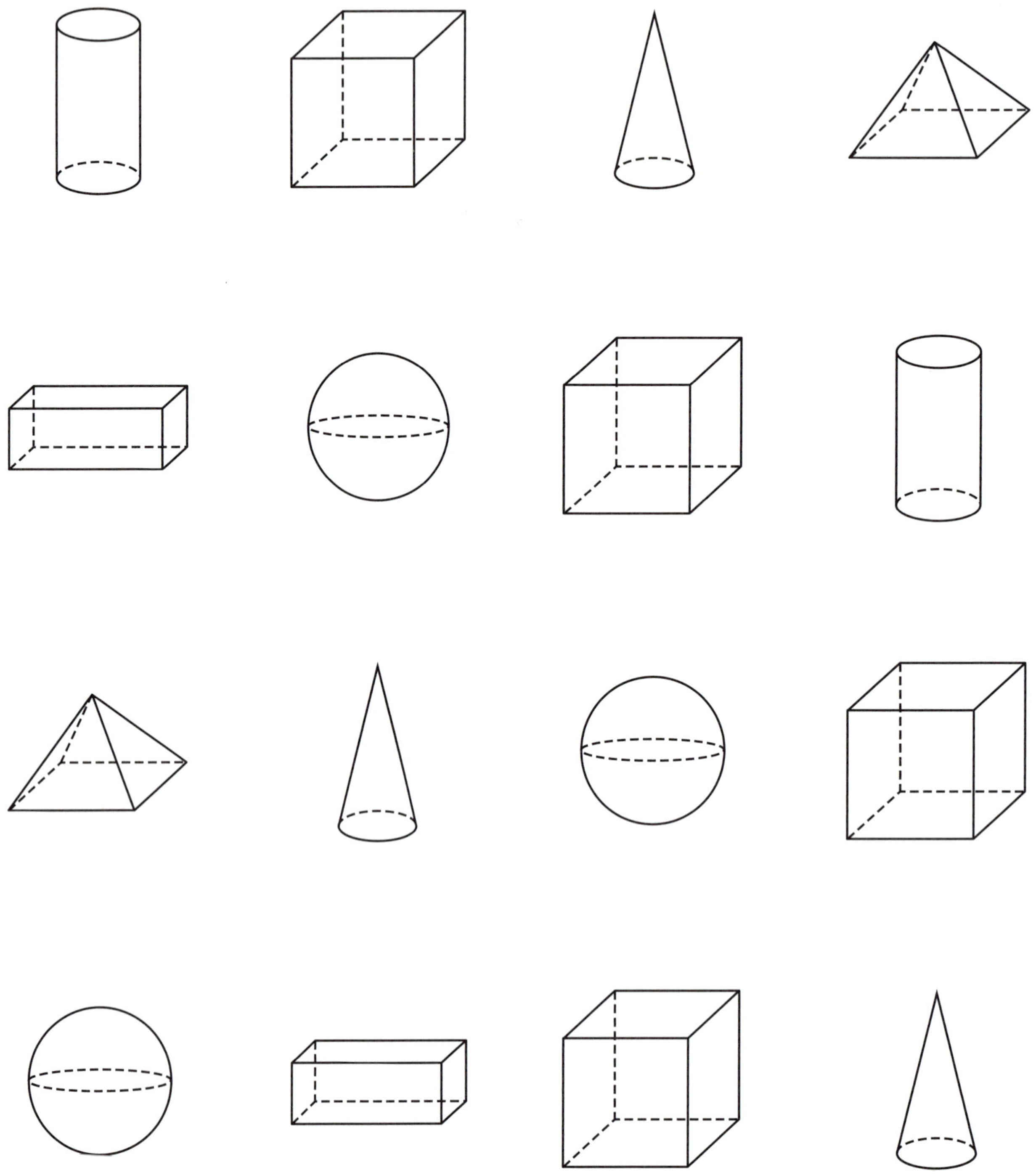

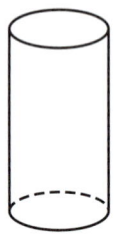

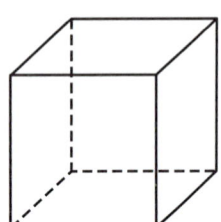

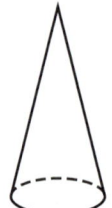

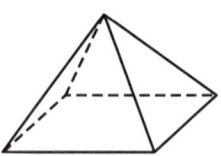

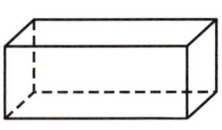

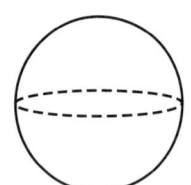

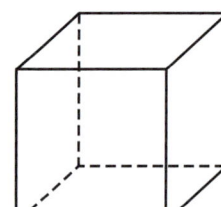

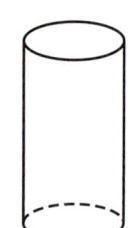

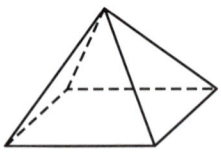

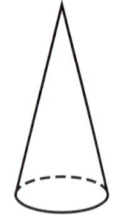

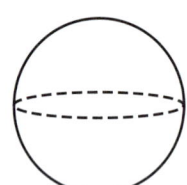

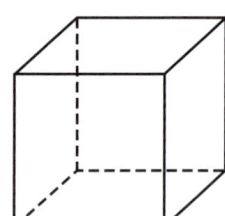

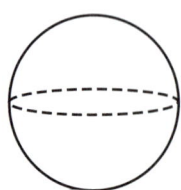

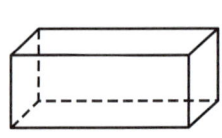

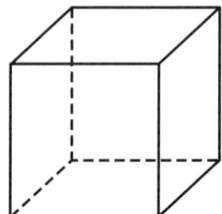

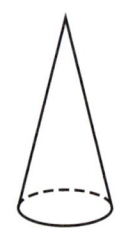

NAME _____

Lesson 1.13
IDENTIFYING 3-D SHAPES: SPHERES

This is a sphere. It looks like a ball.

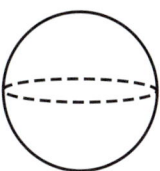

A sphere has curved sides.

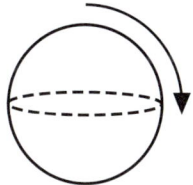

A sphere rolls. It does not stack.

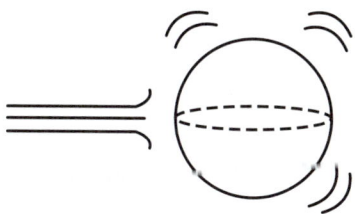

Color the spheres.

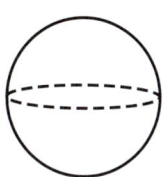 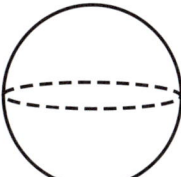 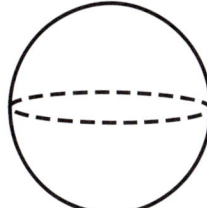

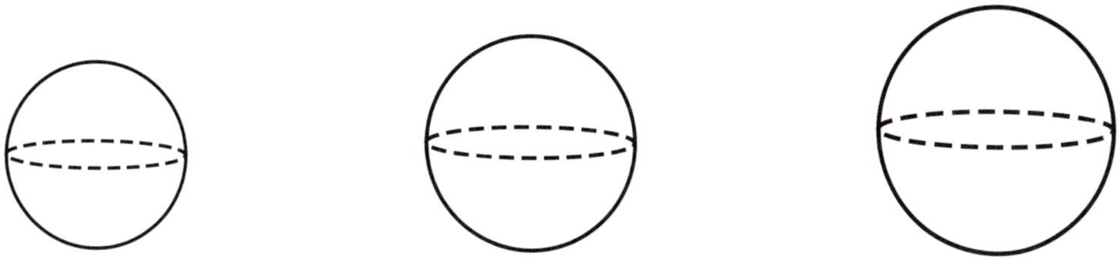

Spectrum Shapes
Kindergarten

Chapter 1, Lesson 13
Identifying Shapes

NAME _____

Lesson 1.13
IDENTIFYING 3-D SHAPES: SPHERES

Put an X on the spheres.

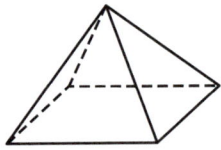 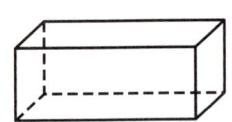  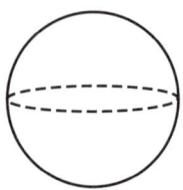

 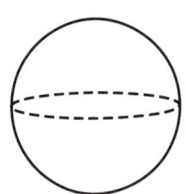 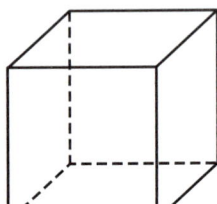 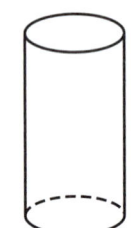

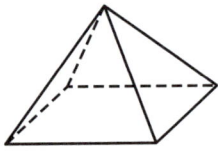  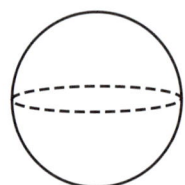 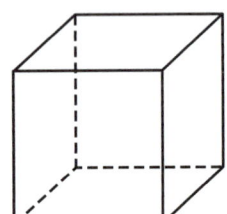

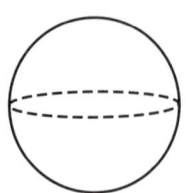  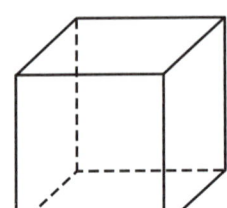 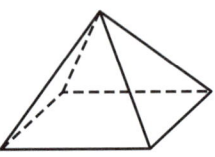

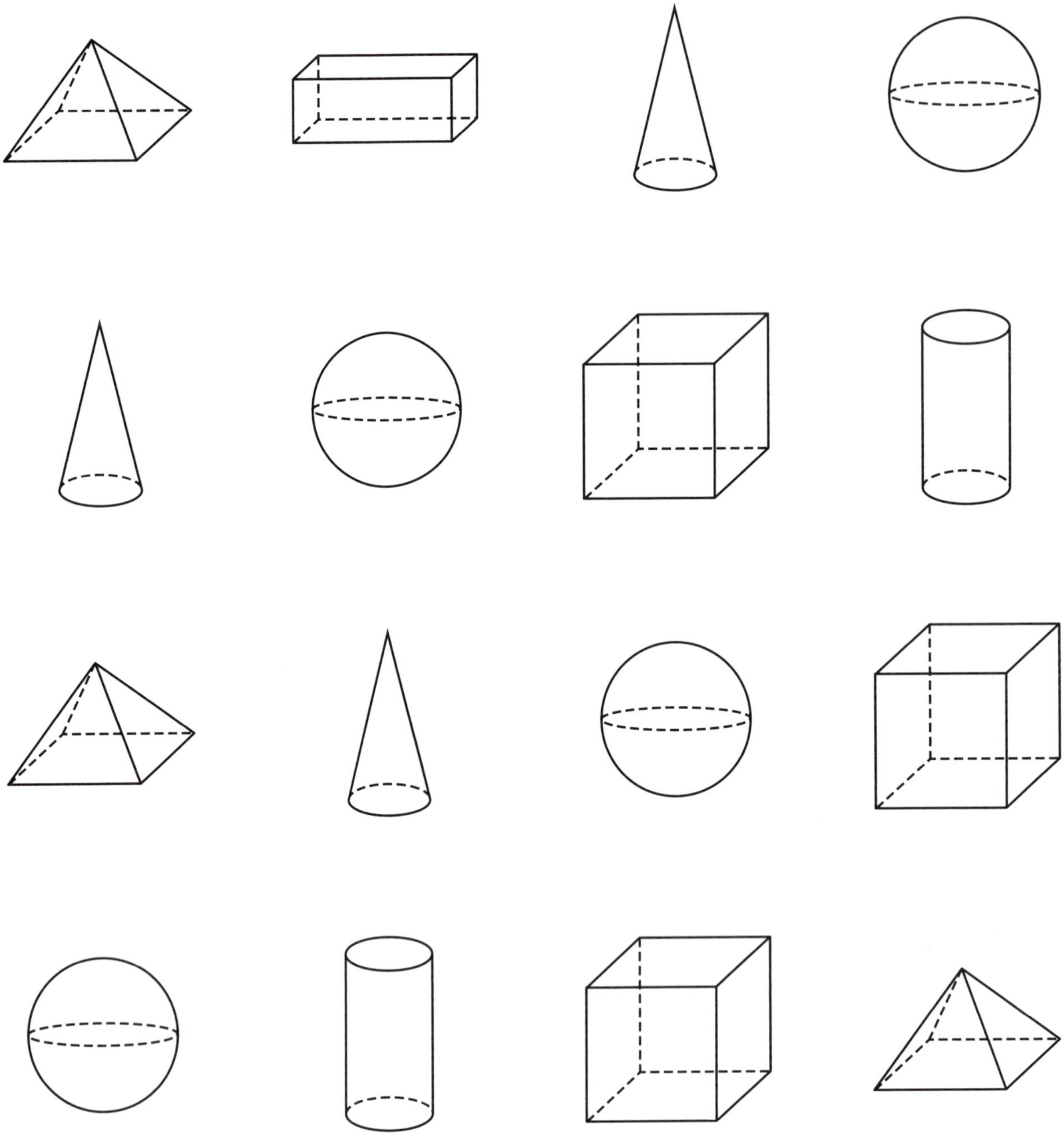

Spectrum Shapes
Kindergarten

Chapter 1, Lesson 13
Identifying Shapes

NAME _____

Lesson 1.14
IDENTIFYING 3-D SHAPES: PYRAMIDS

This is a pyramid.

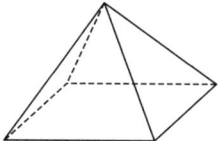

A pyramid has four flat sides or faces.
These faces are shaped like triangles.

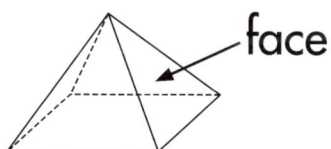

A pyramid also has a face on the bottom.
This face is shaped like a square.

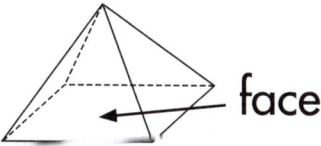

Color the pyramids.

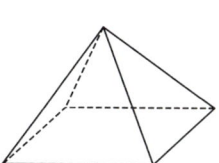 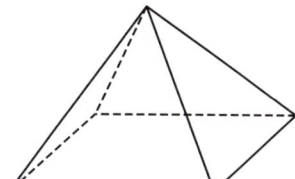 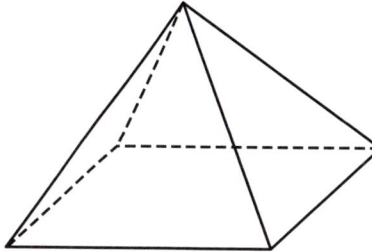

Spectrum Shapes
Kindergarten

Chapter 1, Lesson 14
Identifying Shapes

27

NAME _____

Lesson 1.14
IDENTIFYING 3-D SHAPES: PYRAMIDS

Circle the pyramids.

 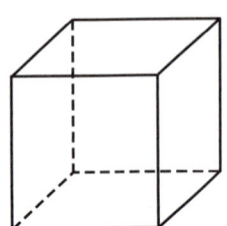 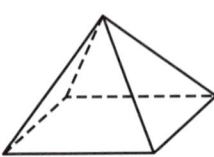 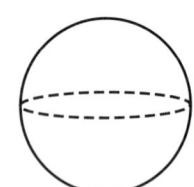

 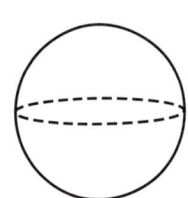 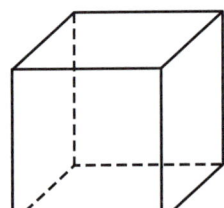 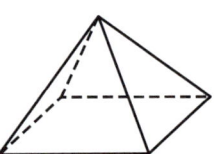

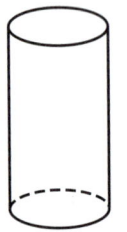 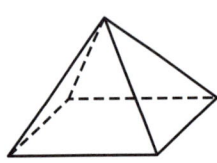 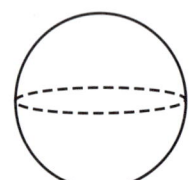 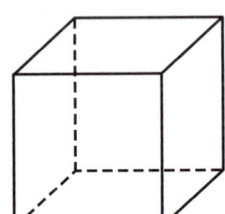

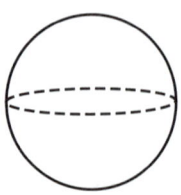 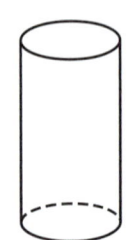 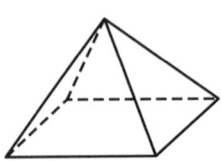 

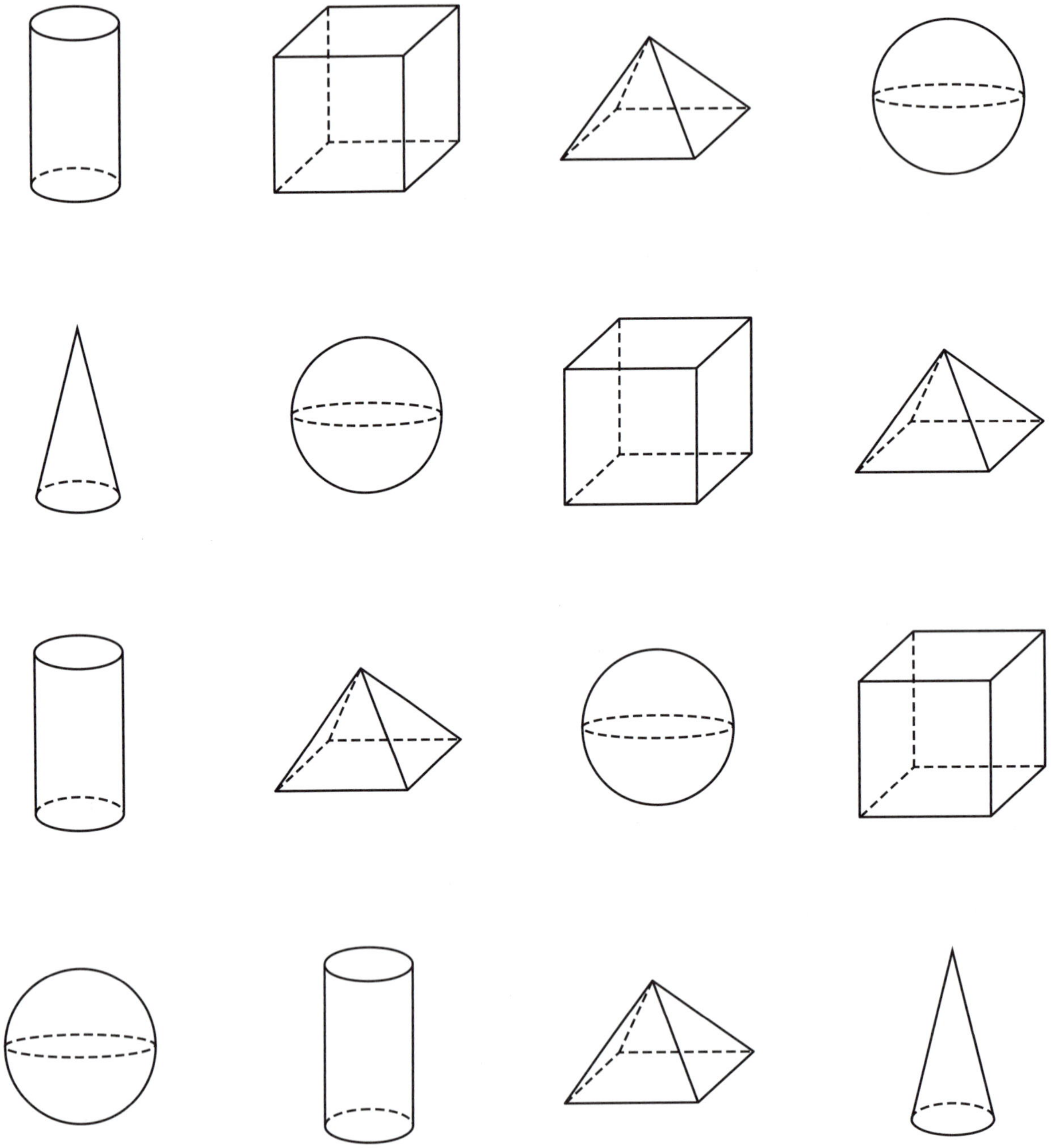

Spectrum Shapes
Kindergarten

Chapter 1, Lesson 14
Identifying Shapes

Lesson 1.15
IDENTIFYING 3-D SHAPES: RECTANGULAR PRISMS

This is a rectangular prism.

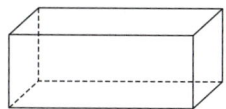

A rectangular prism has six flat sides or faces.

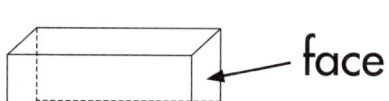

A rectangular prism has eight corners or vertices.

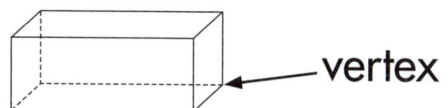

A rectangular prism slides and stacks. It does not roll.

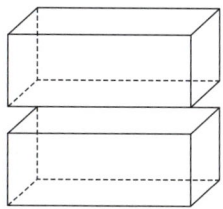 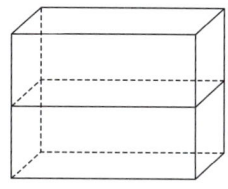

Color the rectangular prisms.

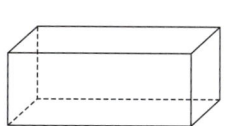 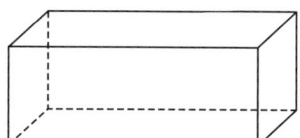 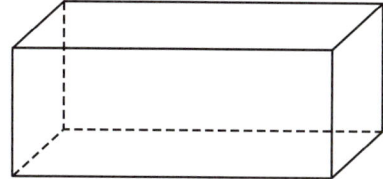

Spectrum Shapes
Kindergarten

Chapter 1, Lesson 15
Identifying Shapes

29

Lesson 1.15
IDENTIFYING 3-D SHAPES: RECTANGULAR PRISMS

Circle the rectangular prisms.

 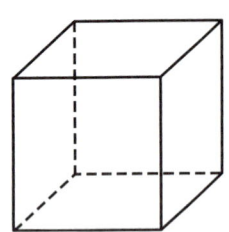  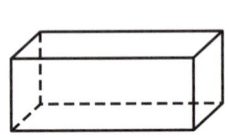

 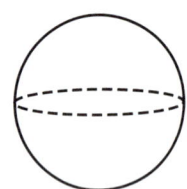 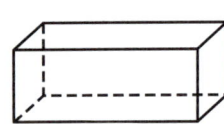 

 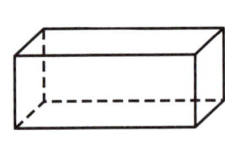 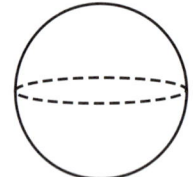 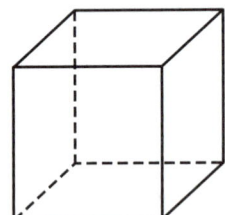

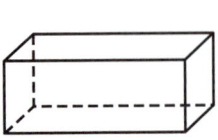 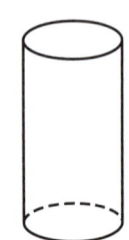 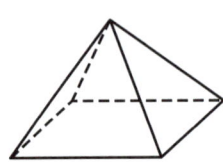 

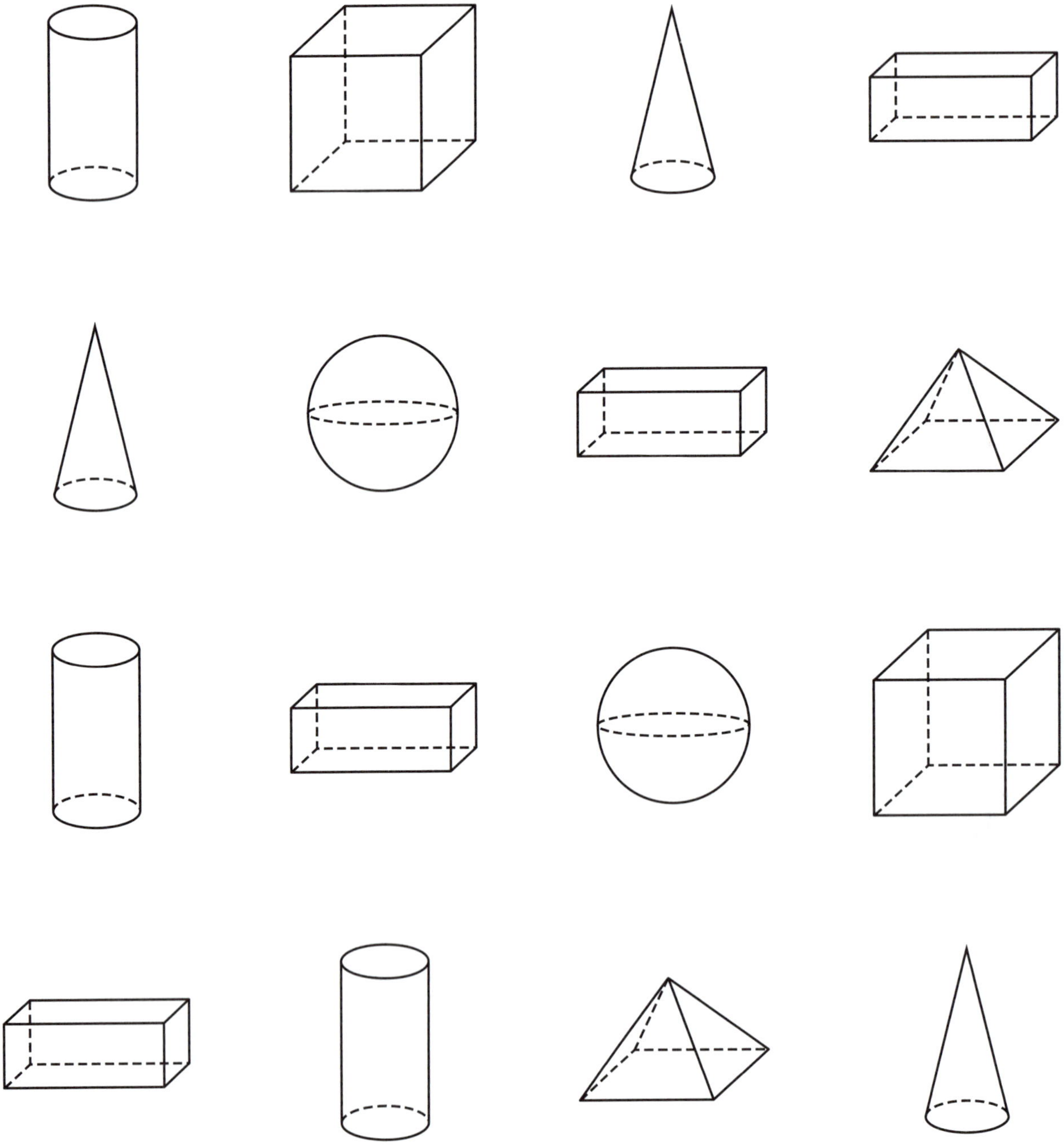

Spectrum Shapes
Kindergarten

Chapter 1, Lesson 15
Identifying Shapes

Lesson 1.16
IDENTIFYING 3-D SHAPES: CONES

This is a cone. It looks like an ice cream cone.

A cone has curved sides.

A cone has a face on the bottom. The face is shaped like a circle.

Color the cones.

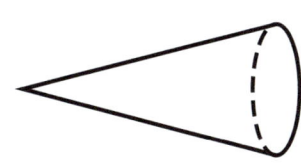

Spectrum Shapes
Kindergarten

Chapter 1, Lesson 16
Identifying Shapes

NAME _____

Lesson 1.16
IDENTIFYING 3-D SHAPES: CONES

Put an X on the cones.

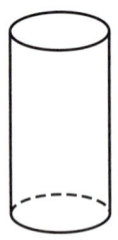 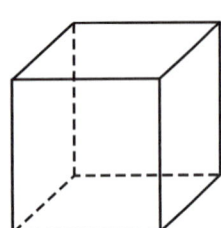  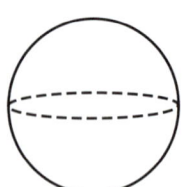

 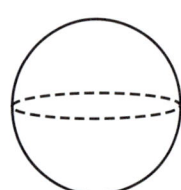 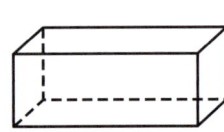 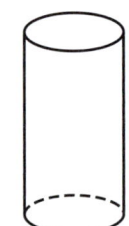

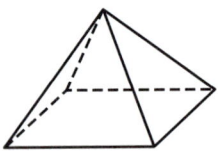  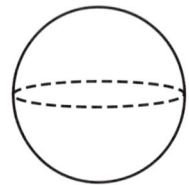 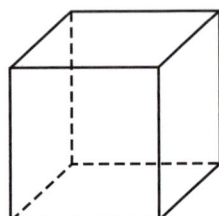

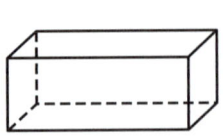  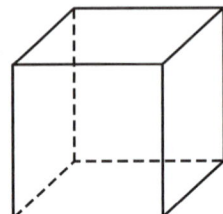 

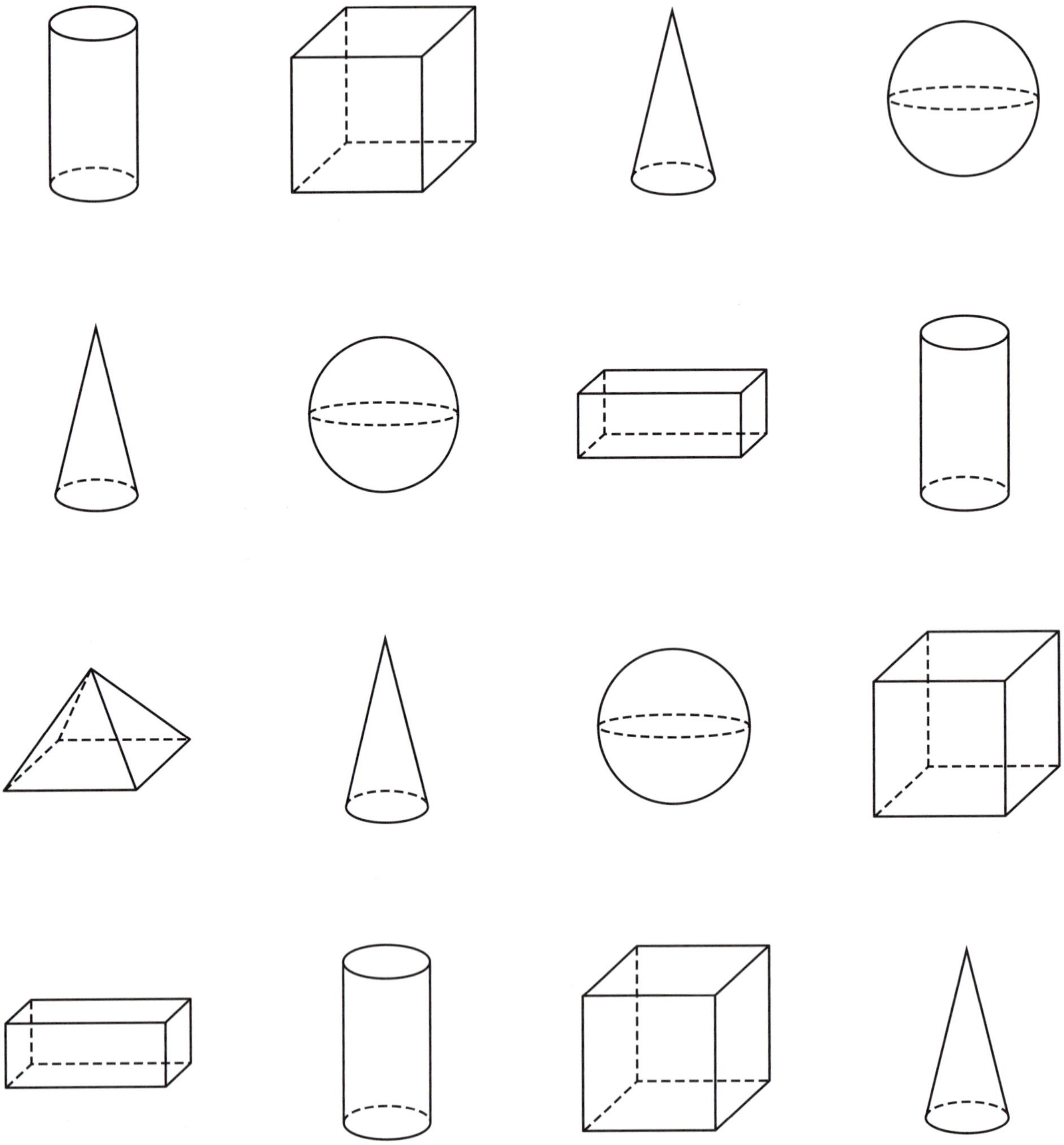

Spectrum Shapes
Kindergarten

Chapter 1, Lesson 16
Identifying Shapes

Lesson 1.17
IDENTIFYING 3-D SHAPES: CYLINDERS

This is a cylinder.

A cylinder has curved sides.

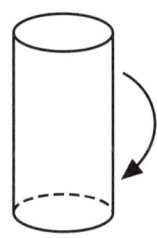

A cylinder has two faces.
The faces are shaped like circles.

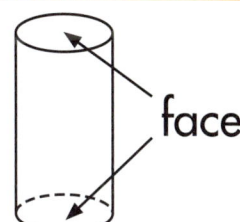

Color the cylinders.

 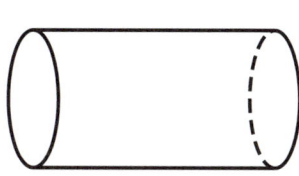 

NAME _____

Lesson 1.17
IDENTIFYING 3-D SHAPES: CYLINDERS

Circle the cylinders.

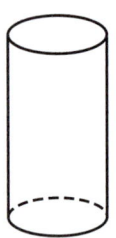 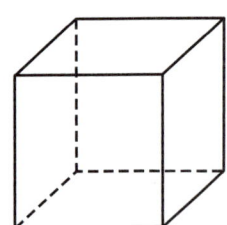  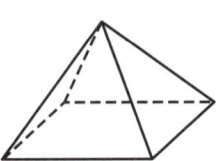

 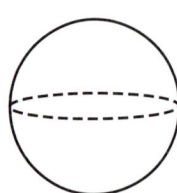 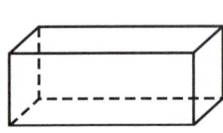 

  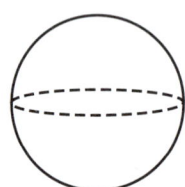 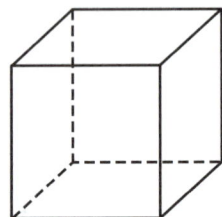

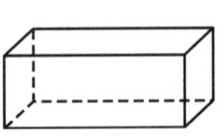 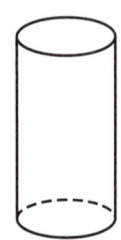 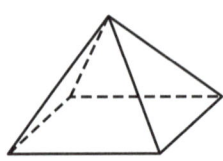 

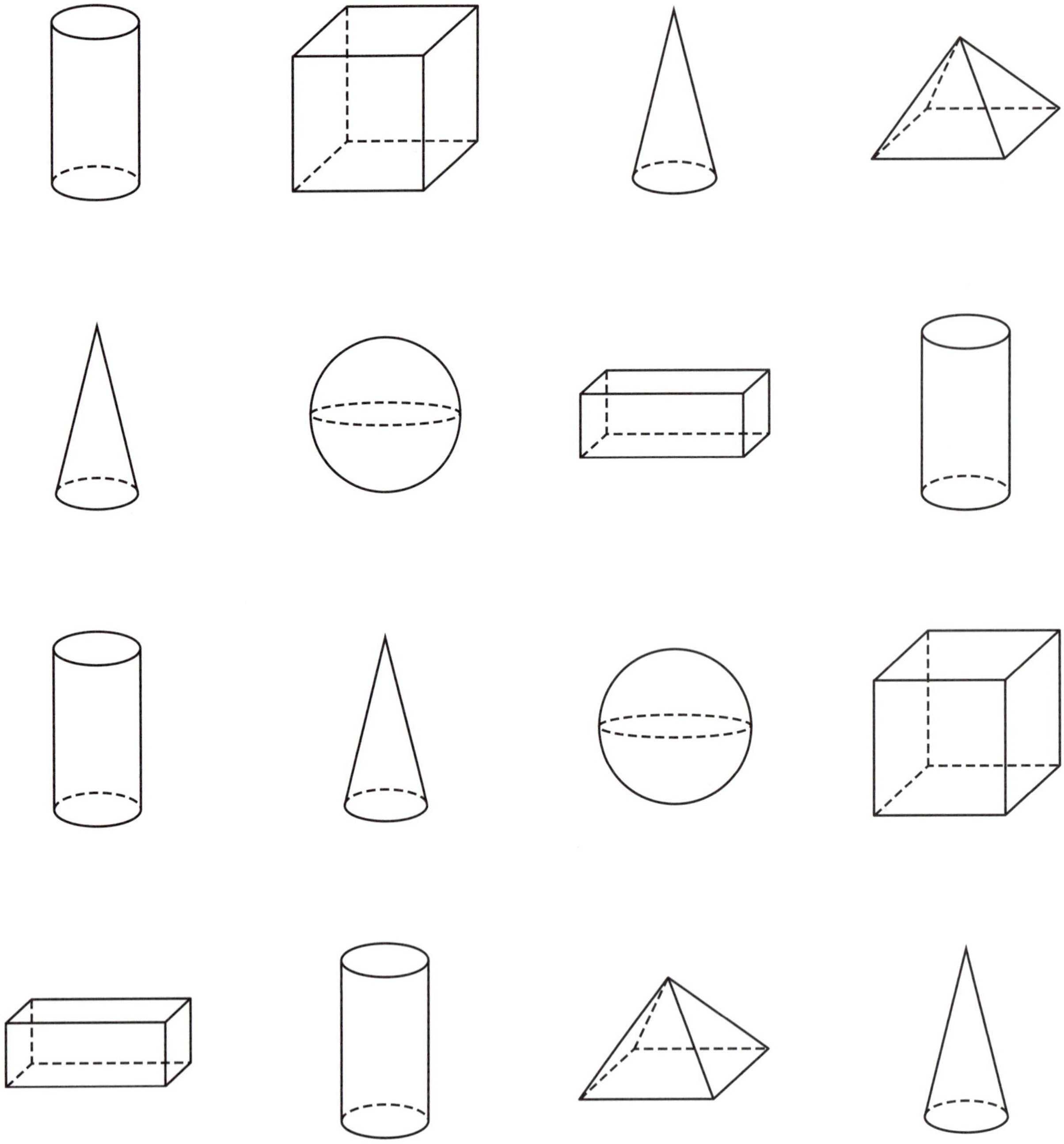

Spectrum Shapes
Kindergarten

Chapter 1, Lesson 17
Identifying Shapes

NAME _____

Lesson 1.18
IDENTIFYING 3-D SHAPES: SAME ORIENTATIONS, SAME SIZES

Color the spheres blue.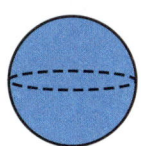

Color the cones red.

Color the cylinders green.

 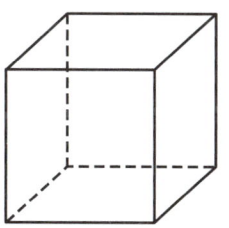  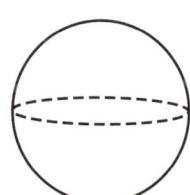

  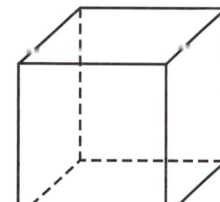 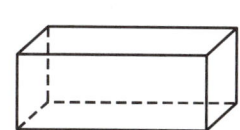

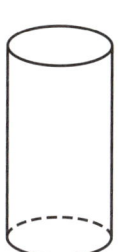  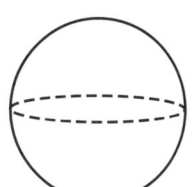 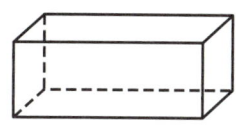

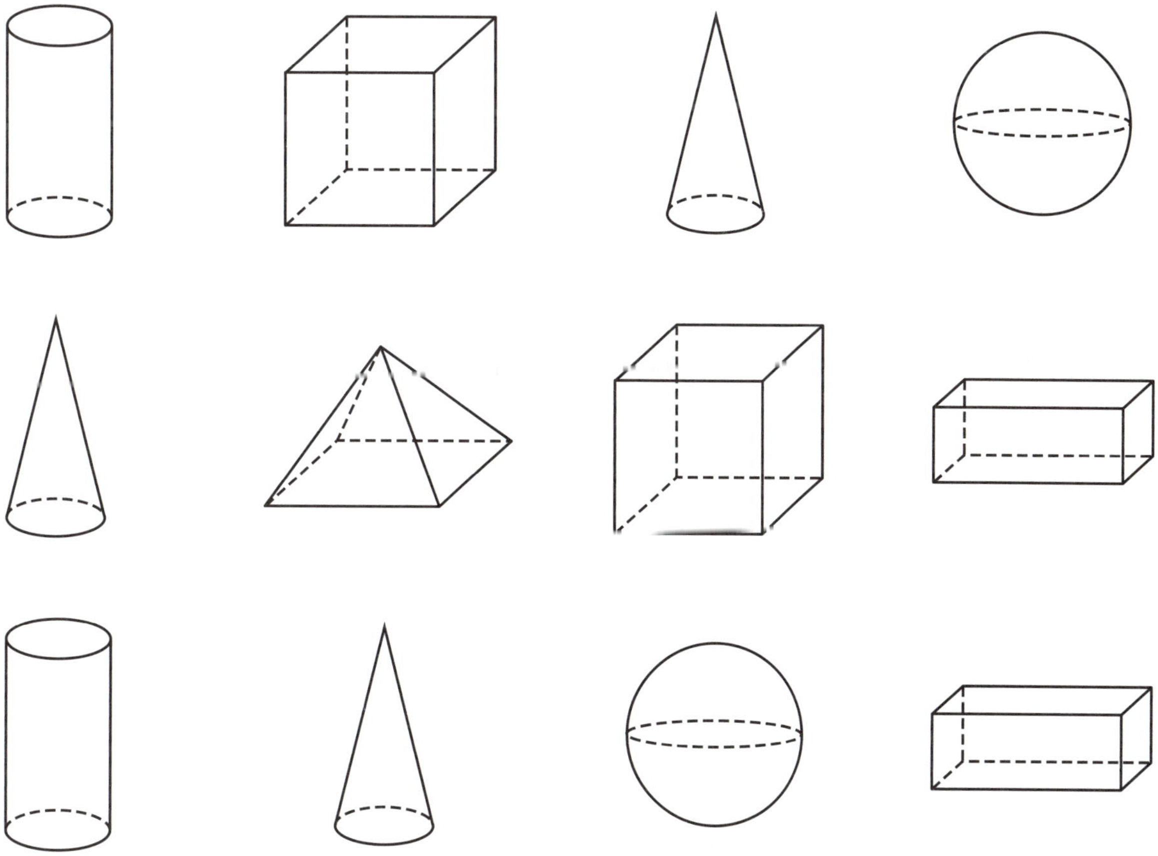

Spectrum Shapes
Kindergarten

Chapter 1, Lesson 18
Identifying Shapes

35

NAME _____

Lesson 1.19
IDENTIFYING 3-D SHAPES: DIFFERENT ORIENTATIONS, SAME SIZES

Color the cubes yellow.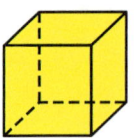

Color the pyramids pink.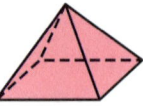

Color the rectangular prisms purple.

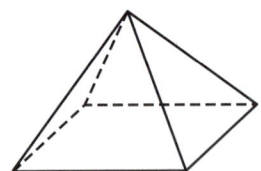 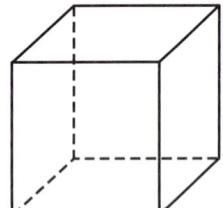  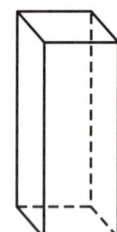

 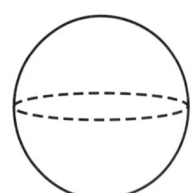 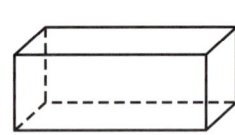 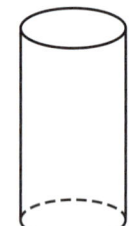

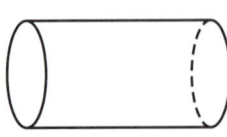 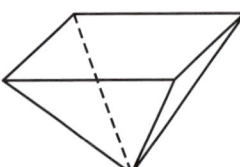 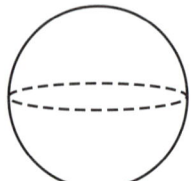 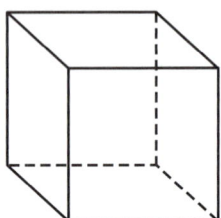

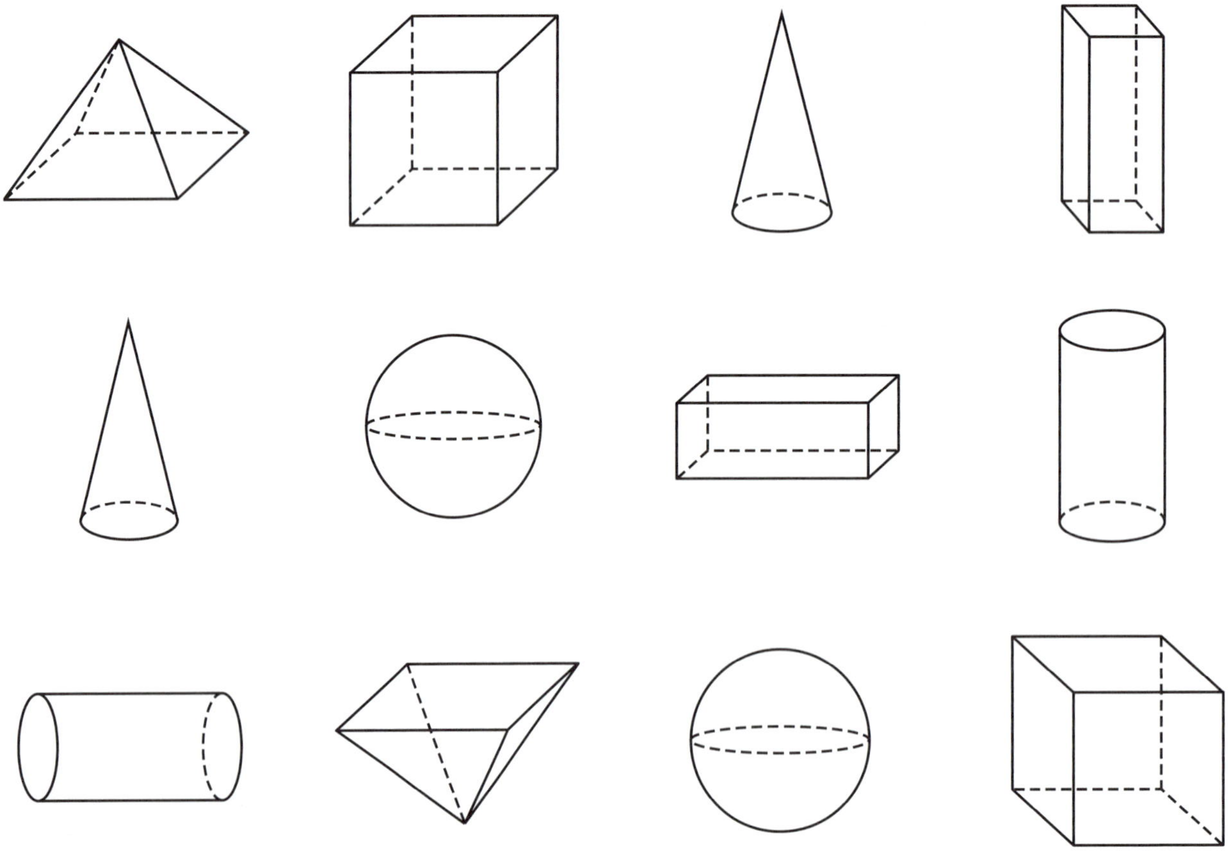

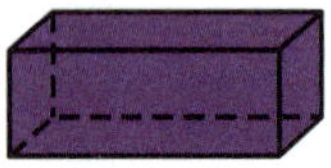

Spectrum Shapes
Kindergarten
36

Chapter 1, Lesson 19
Identifying Shapes

NAME _____

Lesson 1.20
IDENTIFYING 3-D SHAPES: SAME ORIENTATIONS, DIFFERENT SIZES

Color the spheres blue.

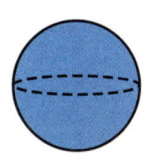

Color the cubes yellow.

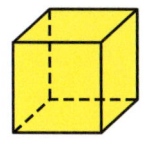

Color the pyramids pink.

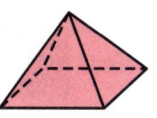

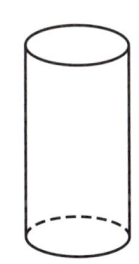

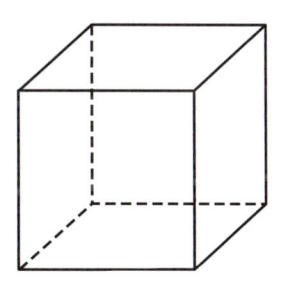

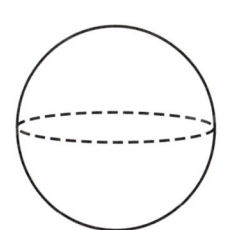

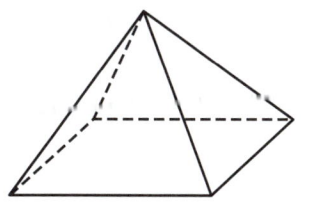

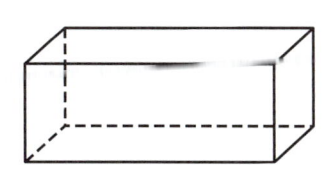

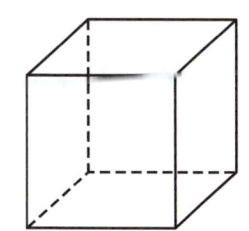

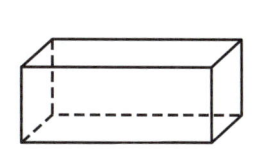

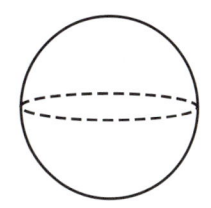

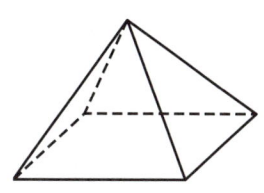

Spectrum Shapes
Kindergarten

Chapter 1, Lesson 20
Identifying Shapes

37

NAME _____

Lesson 1.21
IDENTIFYING 3-D SHAPES: DIFFERENT ORIENTATIONS, DIFFERENT SIZES

Color the cones red.

Color the cylinders green.

Color the rectangular prisms purple.

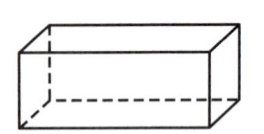

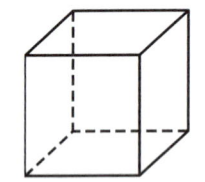

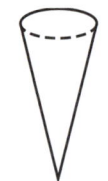

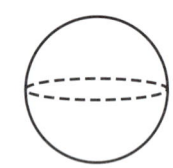

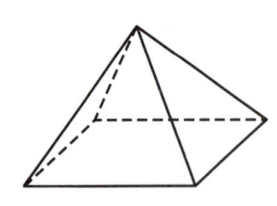

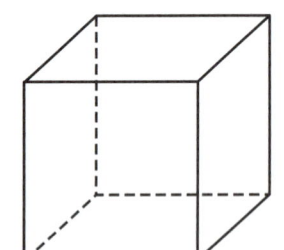

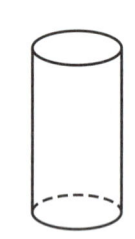

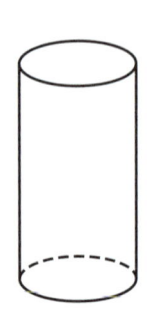

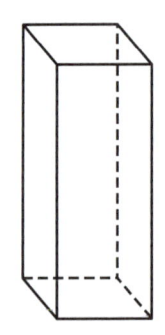

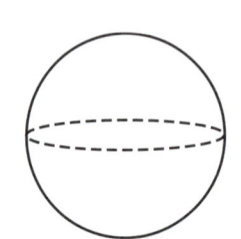

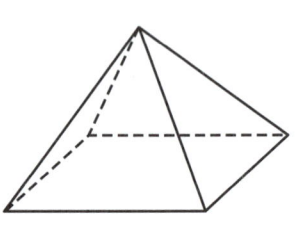

Spectrum Shapes
Kindergarten

Chapter 1, Lesson 21
Identifying Shapes

38

Lesson 1.22
IDENTIFYING 2-D VS. 3-D SHAPES

These are 2-D shapes.

These are 3-D shapes.

Circle the 2-D shapes. Put an X over the 3-D shapes.

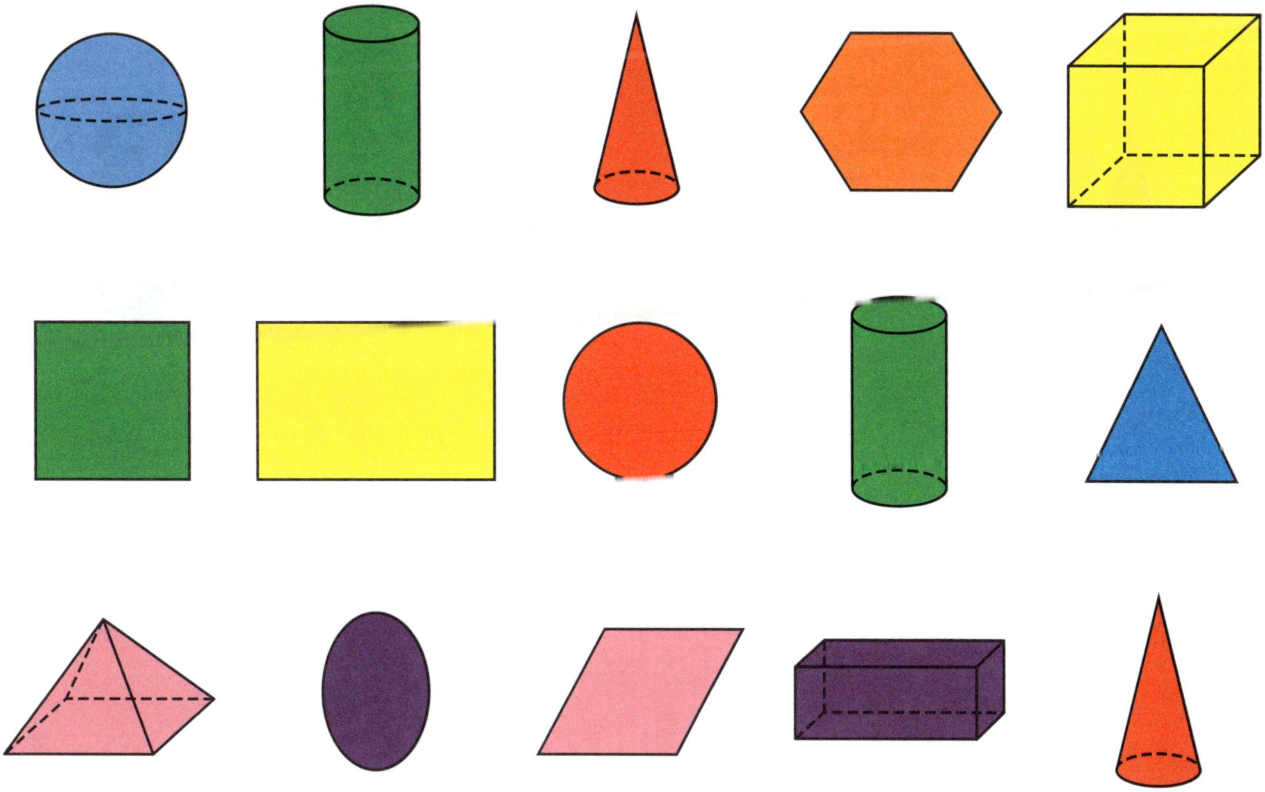

Spectrum Shapes
Kindergarten

Chapter 1, Lesson 22
Identifying Shapes

NAME _____

Lesson 1.22
IDENTIFYING 2-D VS. 3-D SHAPES

Circle the 2-D shapes. Put an X over the 3-D shapes.

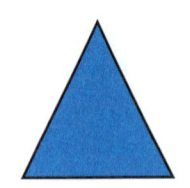

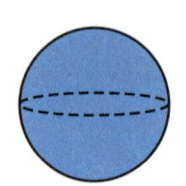

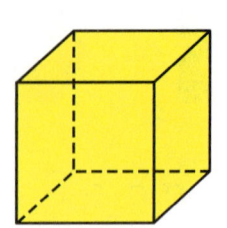

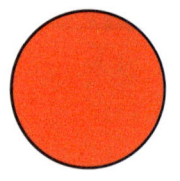

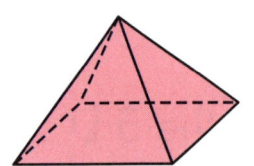

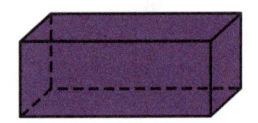

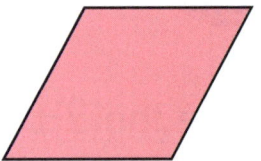

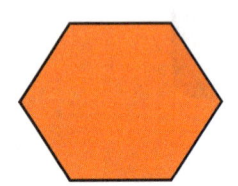

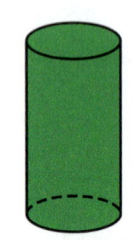

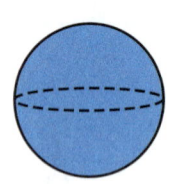

Spectrum Shapes
Kindergarten

Chapter 1, Lesson 22
Identifying Shapes

NAME _____

Lesson 1.22
IDENTIFYING 2-D VS. 3-D SHAPES

Color the 2-D shapes red. Color the 3-D shapes blue.

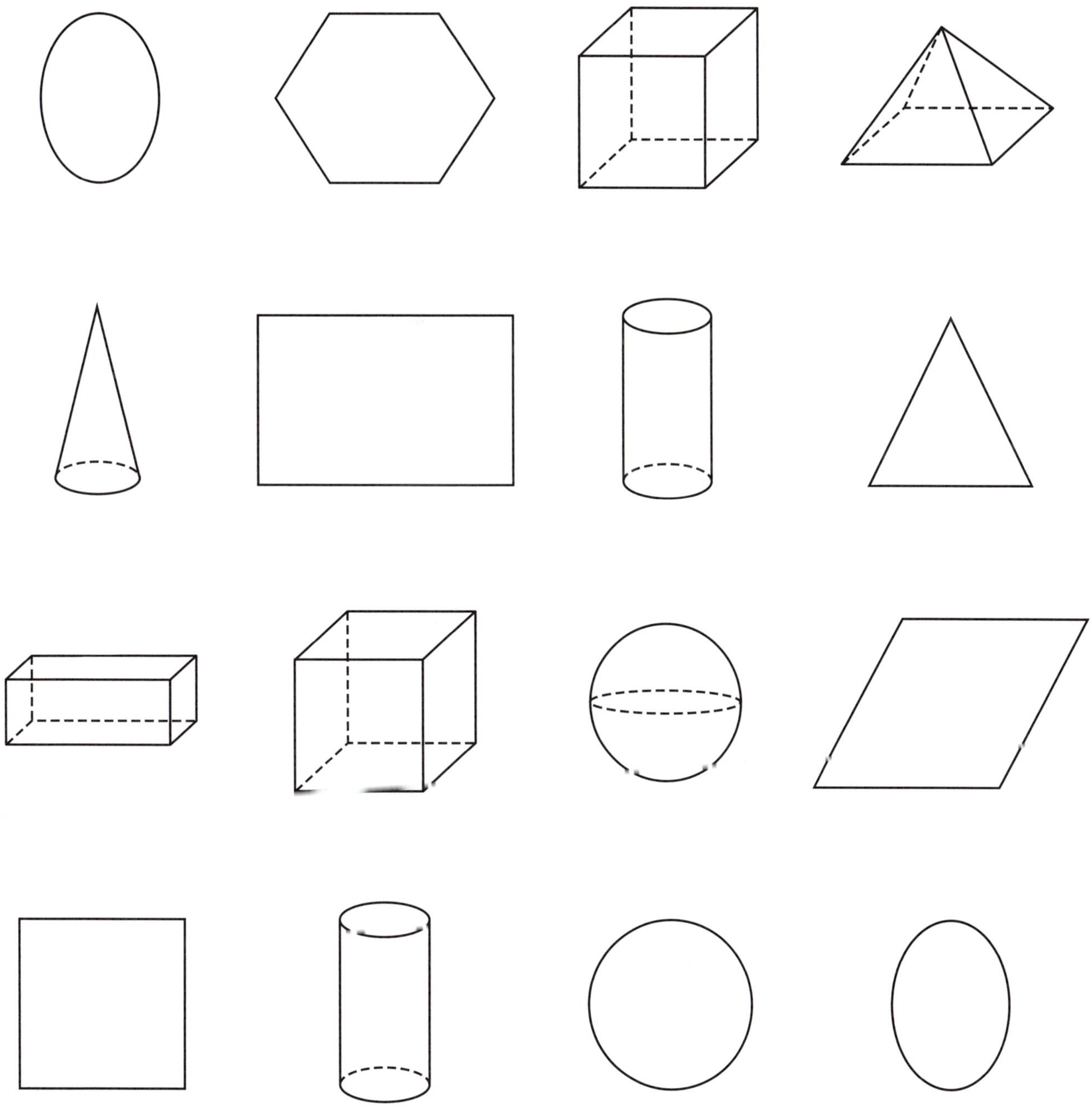

Spectrum Shapes
Kindergarten

Chapter 1, Lesson 22
Identifying Shapes

41

NAME _____

Lesson 1.22
IDENTIFYING 2-D VS. 3-D SHAPES

Circle the 2-D shapes. Put an X over the 3-D shapes.

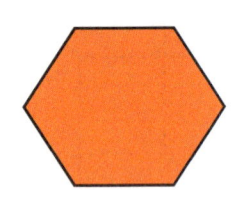

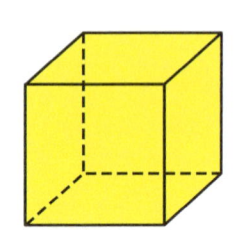

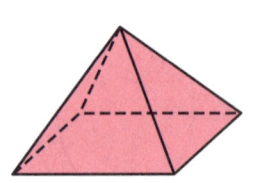

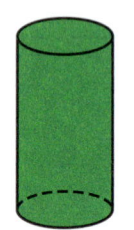

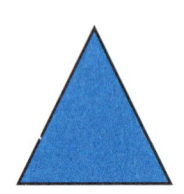

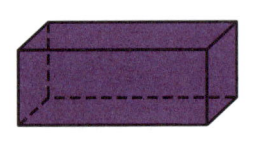

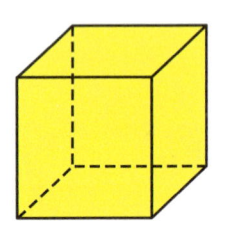

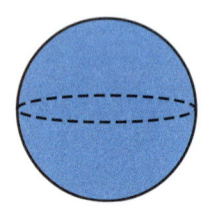

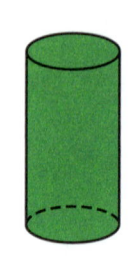

Spectrum Shapes
Kindergarten

42

Chapter 1, Lesson 22
Identifying Shapes

NAME _____

Lesson 2.1
ANALYZING 2-D SHAPES

Circle the shapes that have four sides.

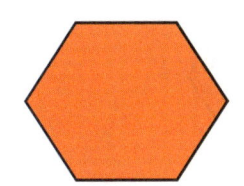

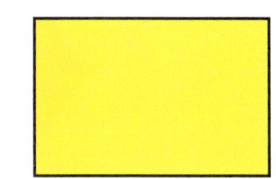

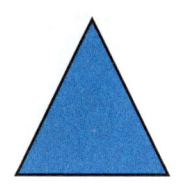

Circle the shape that has three sides.

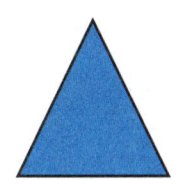

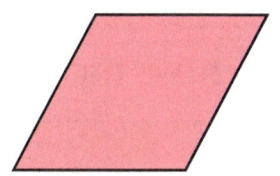

Circle the shapes that have four corners.

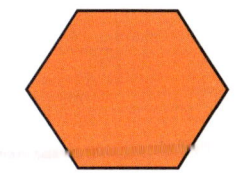

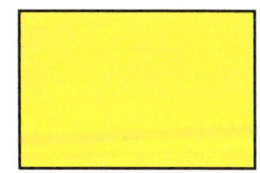

Circle the shape that has four sides of the same length.

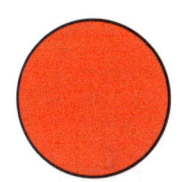

Spectrum Shapes
Kindergarten

Chapter 2, Lesson 1
Analyzing and Comparing Shapes

43

NAME _____

Lesson 2.1
ANALYZING 2-D SHAPES

Tell how many sides the shapes have.

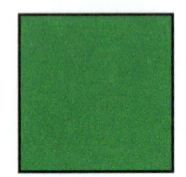

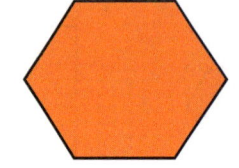

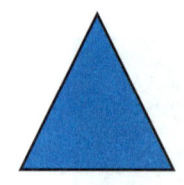

_____ sides   _____ sides   _____ sides

Tell how many corners the shapes have.

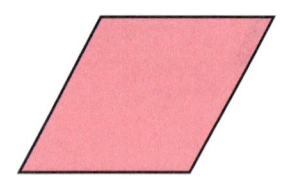

_____ corners   _____ corners   _____ corners

Tell how many sides of the same length the shapes have.

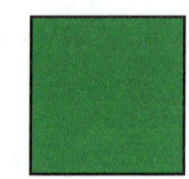

_____ sides of   _____ sides of
equal length   equal length

Spectrum Shapes
Kindergarten

Lesson 2.2
COMPARING 2-D SHAPES

Circle the shapes that have four sides.

Circle the shapes that are curved.

Circle the shapes that have straight sides.

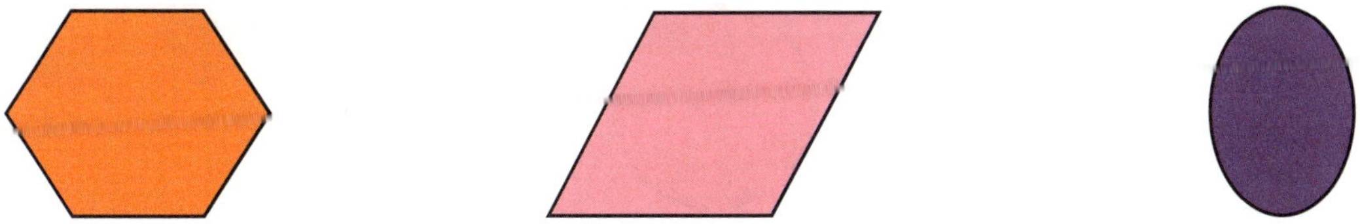

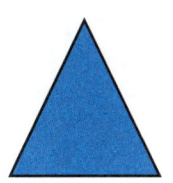

Spectrum Shapes
Kindergarten

Chapter 2, Lesson 2
Analyzing and Comparing Shapes

NAME _____

Lesson 2.2
COMPARING 2-D SHAPES

Cross out the shape that is not curved.

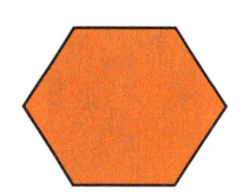

Cross out the shape that does not have four sides.

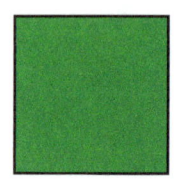

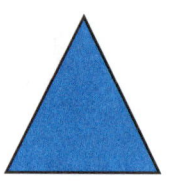

Cross out the shapes that do not have straight sides.

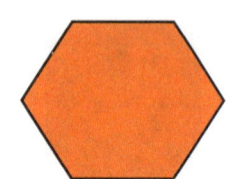

Spectrum Shapes
Kindergarten

Chapter 2, Lesson 2
Analyzing and Comparing Shapes

NAME _____

Lesson 2.3
ANALYZING 3-D SHAPES

Circle the shapes that have six faces.

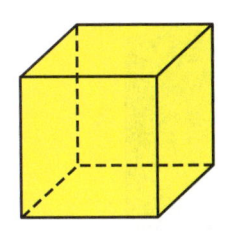

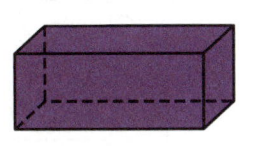

Circle the shape that has no faces.

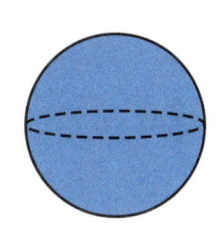

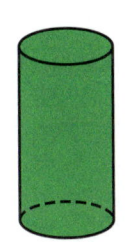

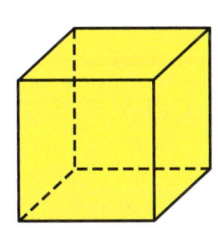

Circle the shapes that roll.

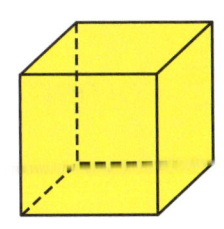

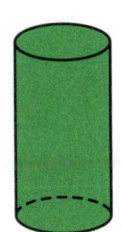

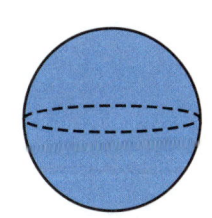

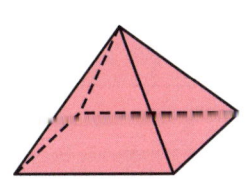

Circle the shapes that stack.

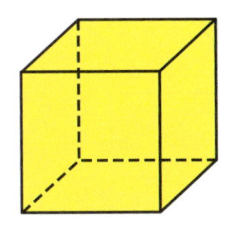

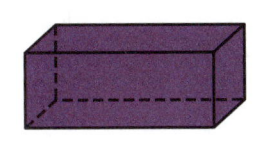

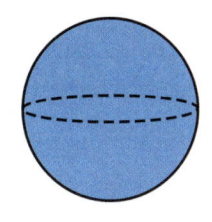

Spectrum Shapes
Kindergarten

Chapter 2, Lesson 3
Analyzing and Comparing Shapes

47

NAME _____

Lesson 2.3
ANALYZING 3-D SHAPES

Tell how many faces the shapes have.

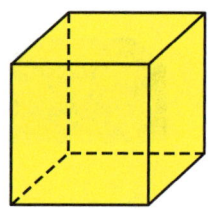

_____ faces   _____ faces   _____ faces

Tell how many corners the shapes have.

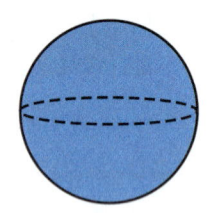

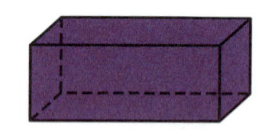

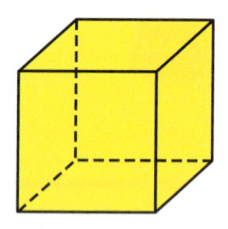

_____ corners   _____ corners   _____ corners

Draw the shape of the faces.

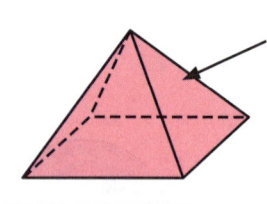

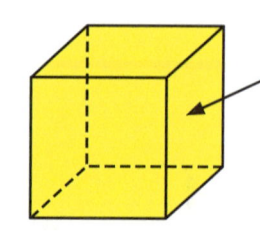

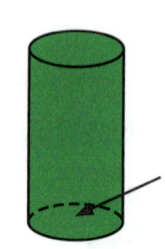

Spectrum Shapes
Kindergarten

Chapter 2, Lesson 3
Analyzing and Comparing Shapes

NAME _____

Lesson 2.4
COMPARING 3-D SHAPES

Circle the shapes that have square faces.

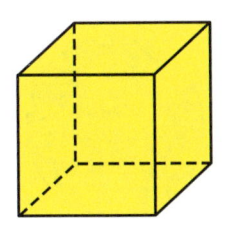

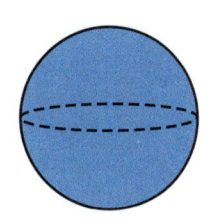

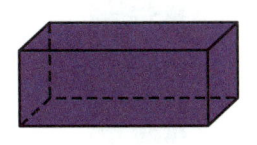

Circle the shapes that have circles for faces.

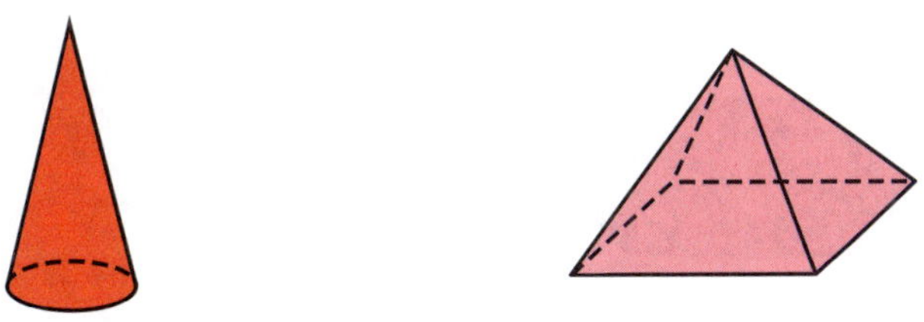

Circle the shapes that both stack and roll.

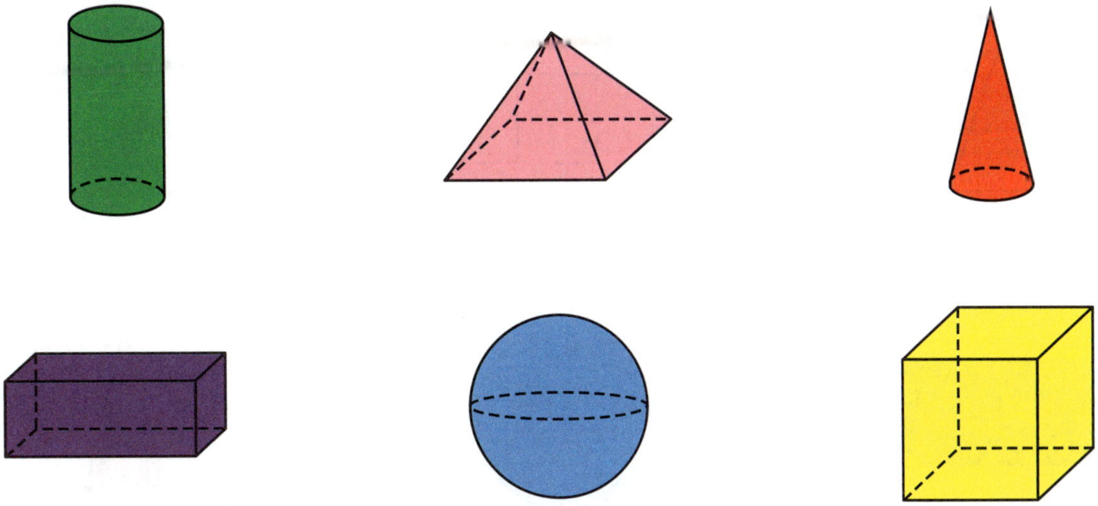

Spectrum Shapes
Kindergarten

Chapter 2, Lesson 4
Analyzing and Comparing Shapes

NAME _____

Lesson 2.4
COMPARING 3-D SHAPES

Cross out the shape that does not stack.

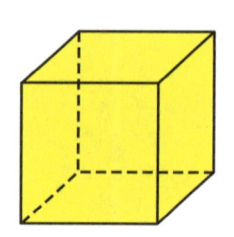

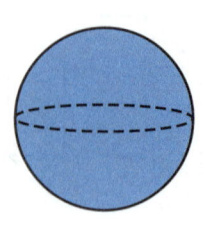

Cross out the shape that does not have curved sides.

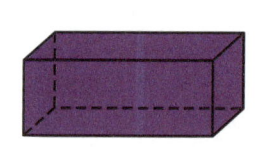

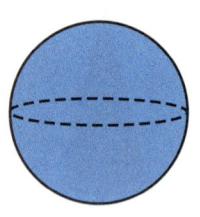

Cross out the shapes that do not have a square face.

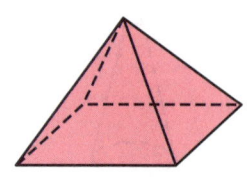

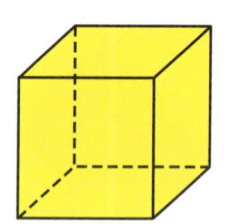

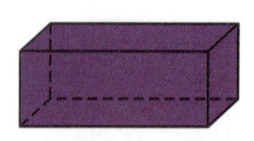

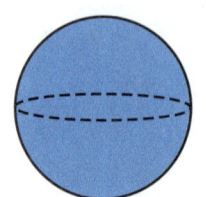

Spectrum Shapes
Kindergarten

Chapter 2, Lesson 4
Analyzing and Comparing Shapes

NAME _____

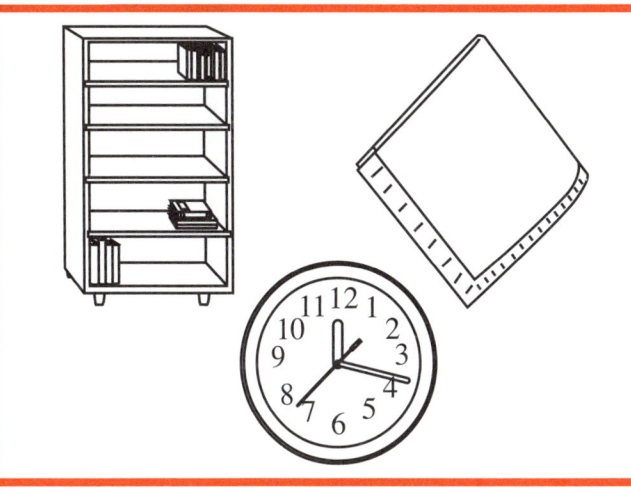

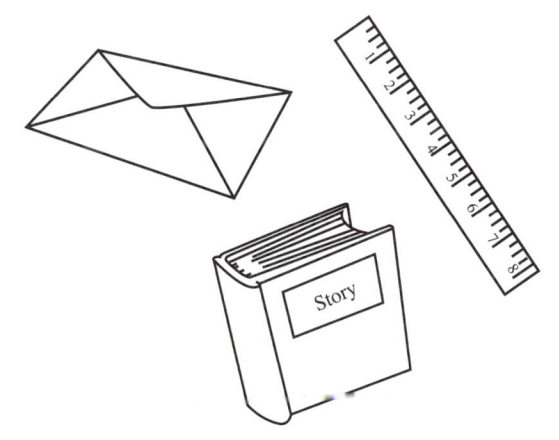

Lesson 3.1
IDENTIFYING 2-D SHAPES WITHIN PICTURES: SQUARES

Color the square shapes green.

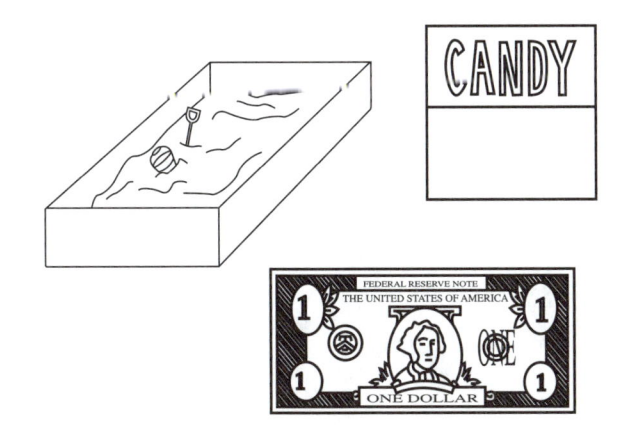

Spectrum Shapes
Kindergarten

Chapter 3, Lesson 1
Identifying Shapes within Pictures

51

NAME _____

Lesson 3.2
IDENTIFYING 2-D SHAPES WITHIN PICTURES: CIRCLES

Color the circle shapes red.

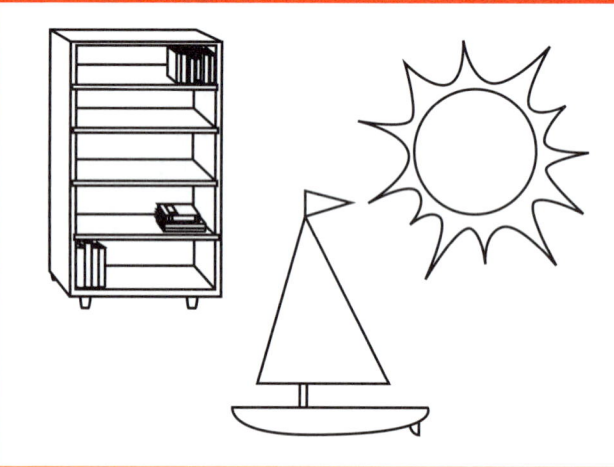

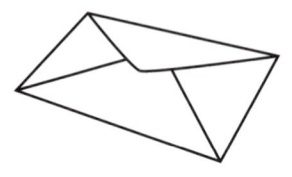

Spectrum Shapes
Kindergarten

Chapter 3, Lesson 2
Identifying Shapes within Pictures

NAME _____

Lesson 3.3
IDENTIFYING 2-D SHAPES WITHIN PICTURES: TRIANGLES

Color the triangle shapes blue.

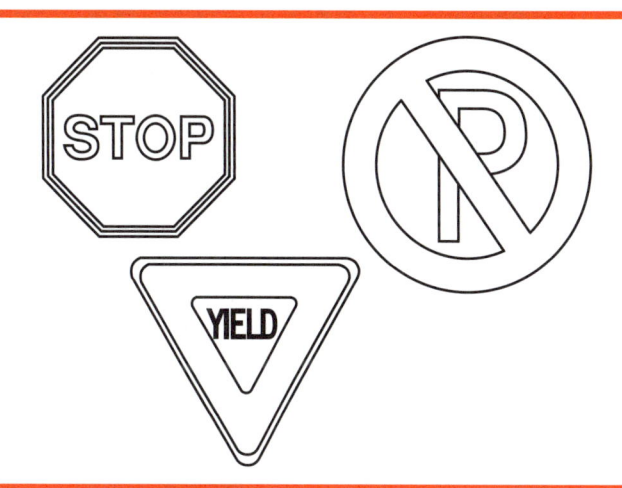

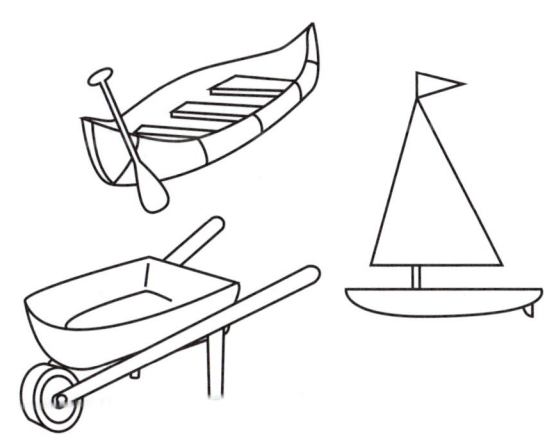

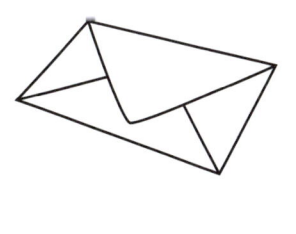

Spectrum Shapes
Kindergarten

Chapter 3, Lesson 3
Identifying Shapes within Pictures

53

NAME _____

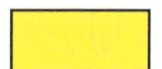

Lesson 3.4
IDENTIFYING 2-D SHAPES WITHIN PICTURES: RECTANGLES

Color the rectangle shapes yellow.

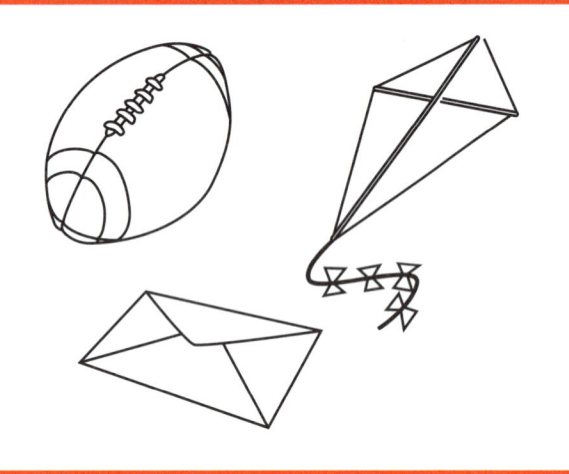

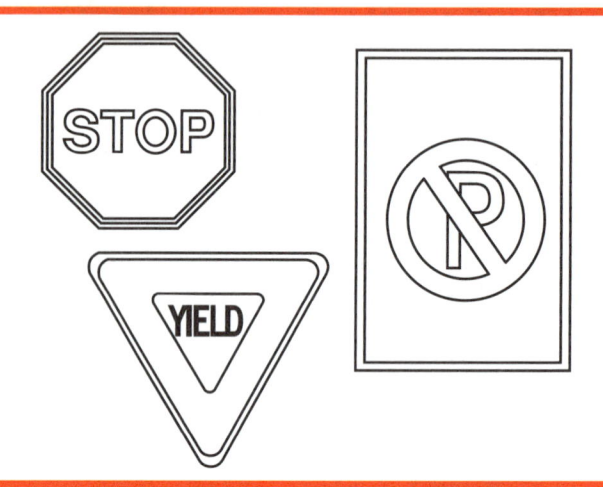

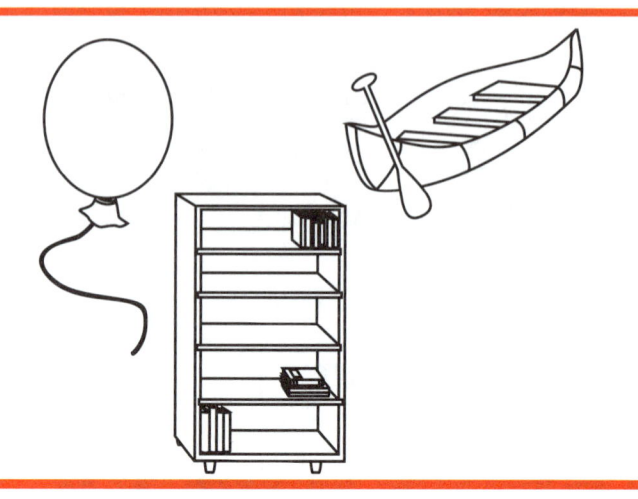

Spectrum Shapes
Kindergarten
54

Chapter 3, Lesson 4
Identifying Shapes within Pictures

NAME _____

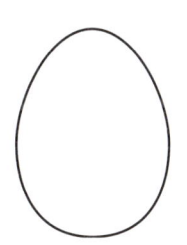

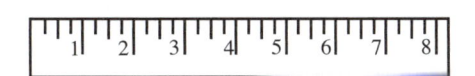

Lesson 3.5
IDENTIFYING 2-D SHAPES WITHIN PICTURES: OVALS

Color the oval shapes purple.

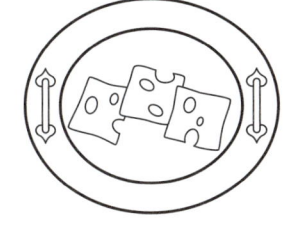

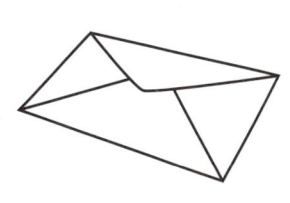

Spectrum Shapes
Kindergarten

Chapter 3, Lesson 5
Identifying Shapes within Pictures

55

NAME _____

Lesson 3.6
IDENTIFYING 2-D SHAPES WITHIN PICTURES: RHOMBUSES

Color the rhombus shapes pink.

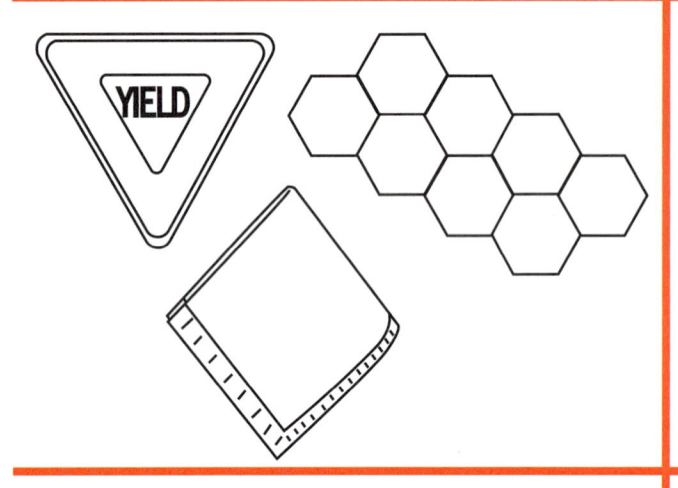

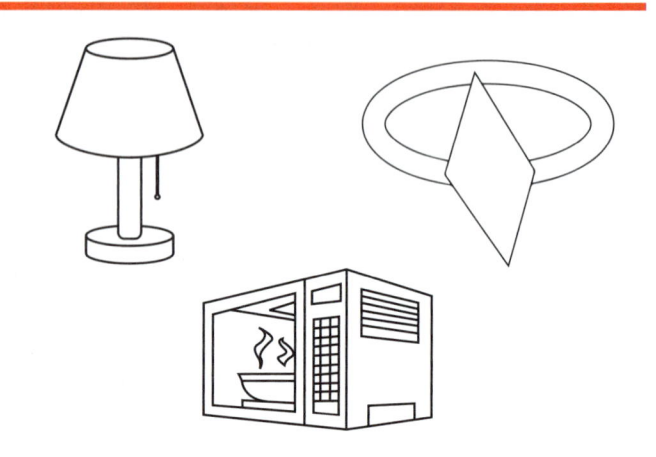

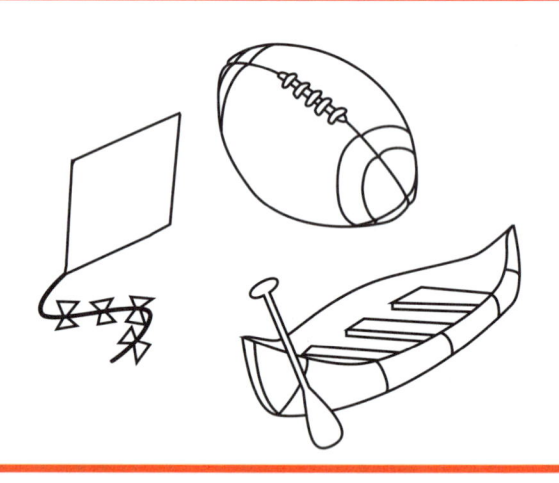

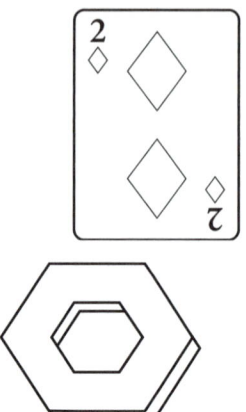

Spectrum Shapes
Kindergarten
56

Chapter 3, Lesson 6
Identifying Shapes within Pictures

NAME _____

Lesson 3.7
IDENTIFYING 2-D SHAPES WITHIN PICTURES: HEXAGONS

Color the hexagon shapes orange.

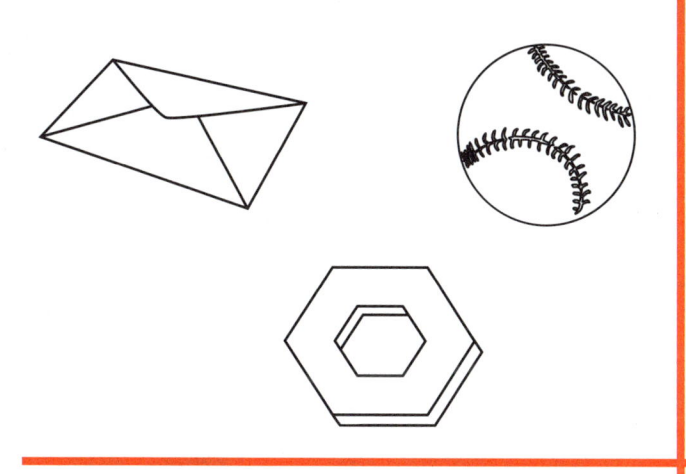

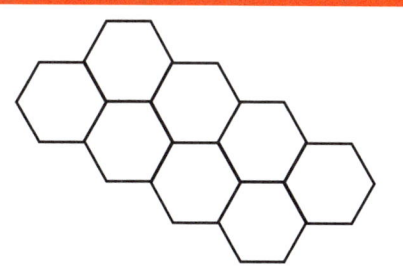

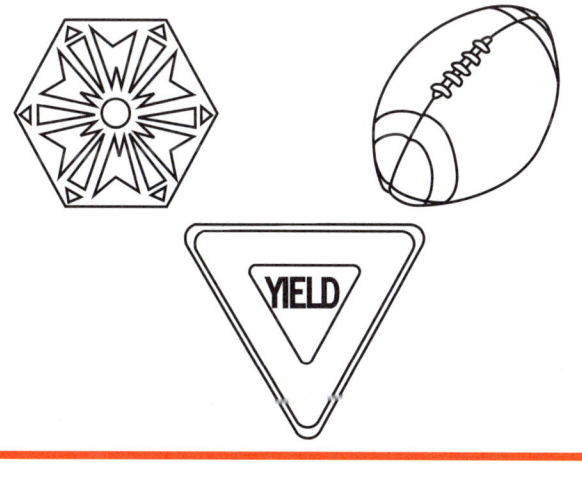

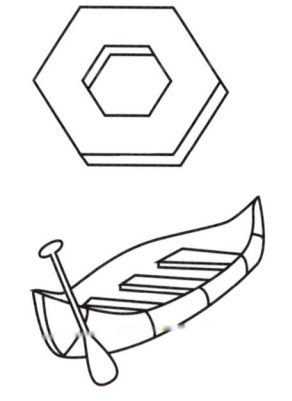

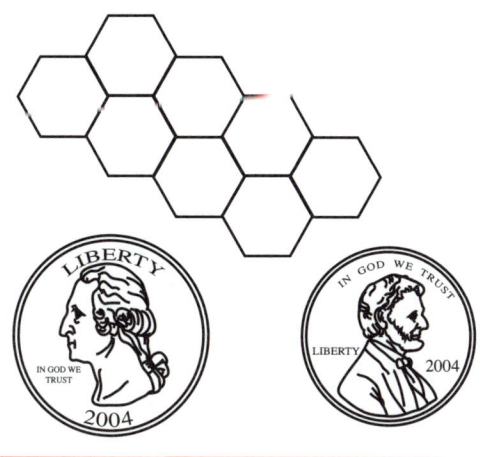

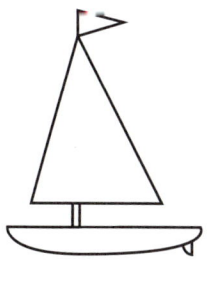

Spectrum Shapes
Kindergarten

Chapter 3, Lesson 7
Identifying Shapes within Pictures

57

NAME _____

Lesson 3.8
IDENTIFYING 3-D SHAPES WITHIN PICTURES: CUBES

Color the cube shapes yellow.

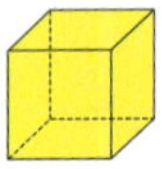

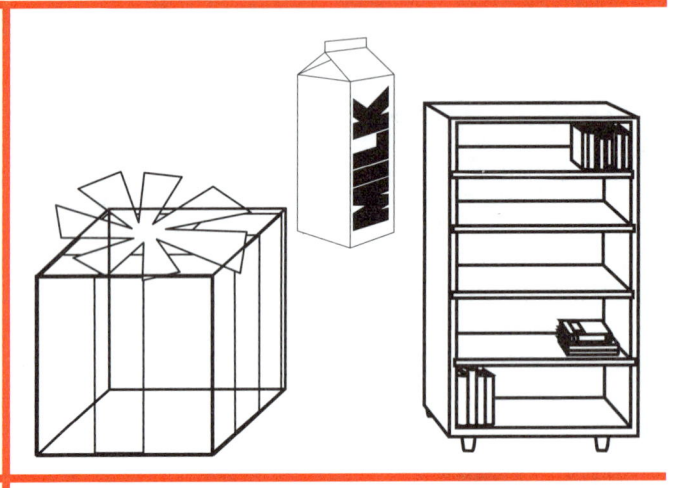

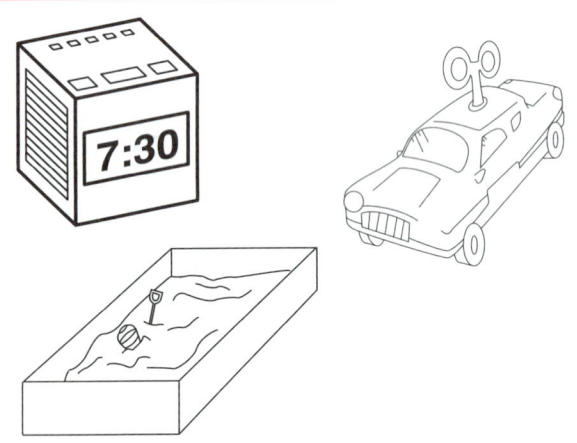

Spectrum Shapes
Kindergarten
58

Chapter 3, Lesson 8
Identifying Shapes within Pictures

NAME _____

Lesson 3.9
IDENTIFYING 3-D SHAPES WITHIN PICTURES: SPHERES

Color the sphere shapes blue.

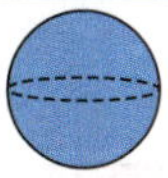

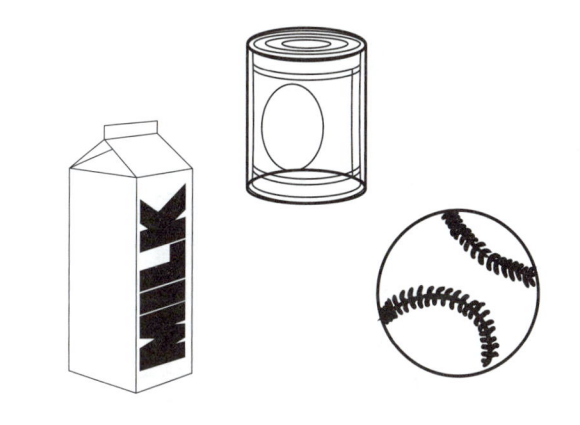

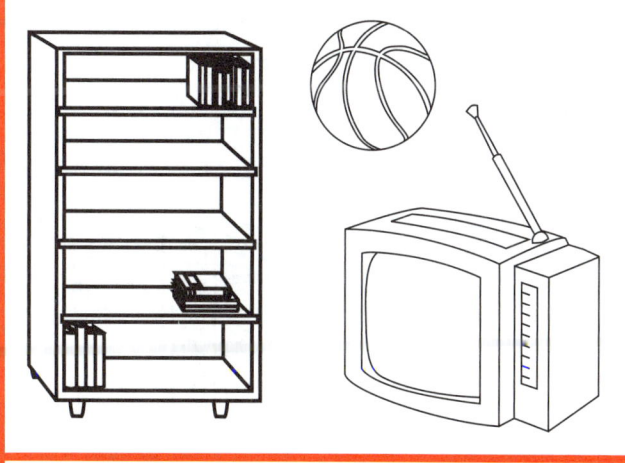

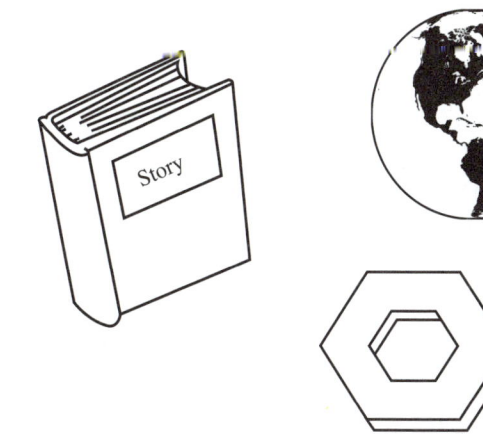

Spectrum Shapes
Kindergarten

Chapter 3, Lesson 9
Identifying Shapes within Pictures

59

NAME _____

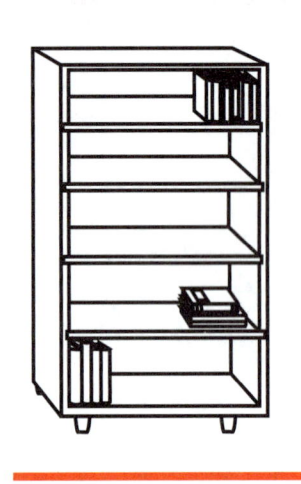

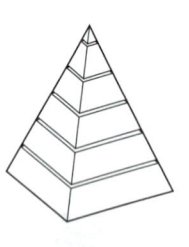

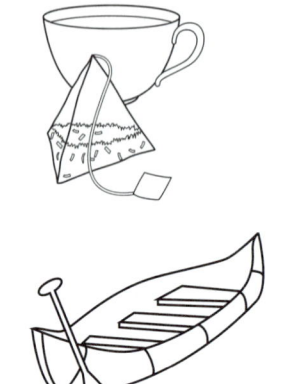

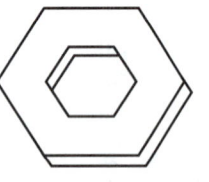

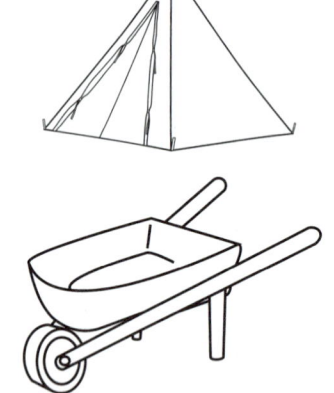

Lesson 3.10
IDENTIFYING 3-D SHAPES WITHIN PICTURES: PYRAMIDS

Color the pyramid shapes pink.

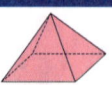

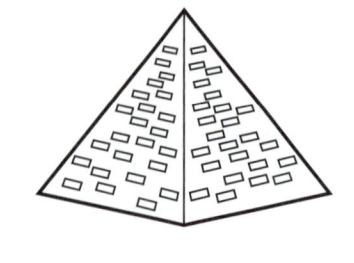

Spectrum Shapes
Kindergarten

Chapter 3, Lesson 10
Identifying Shapes within Pictures

NAME _____

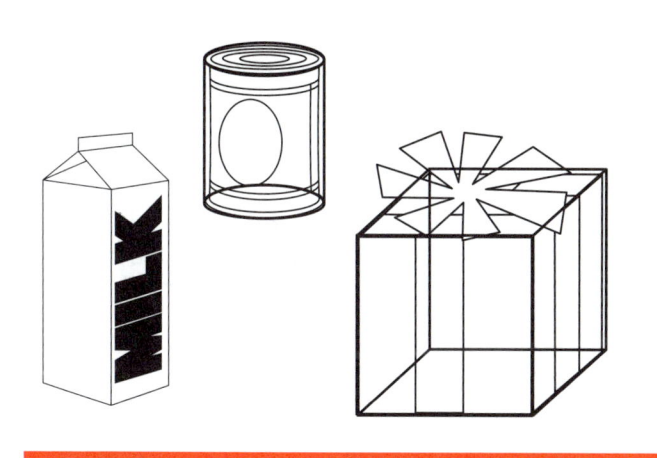

Lesson 3.11
IDENTIFYING 3-D SHAPES WITHIN PICTURES: RECTANGULAR PRISMS

Color the rectangular prism shapes purple.

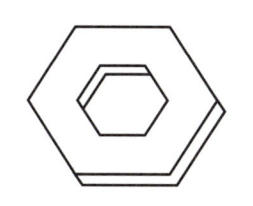

Spectrum Shapes
Kindergarten

Chapter 3, Lesson 11
Identifying Shapes within Pictures

61

Lesson 3.12
IDENTIFYING 3-D SHAPES WITHIN PICTURES: CONES

Color the cone shapes red.

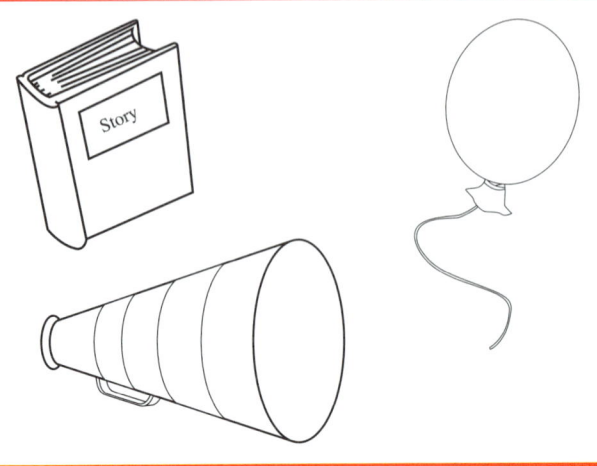

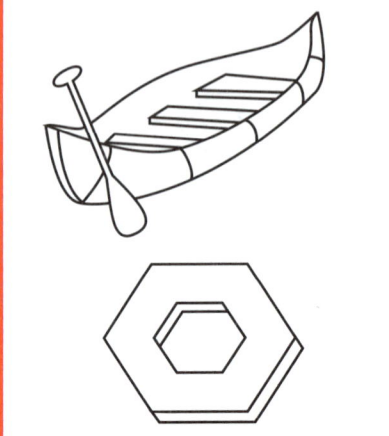

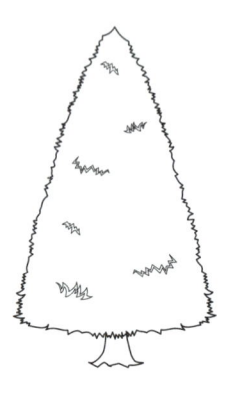

Spectrum Shapes
Kindergarten

Chapter 3, Lesson 12
Identifying Shapes within Pictures

NAME _____

Lesson 3.13
IDENTIFYING 3-D SHAPES WITHIN PICTURES: CYLINDERS

Color the cylinder shapes green.

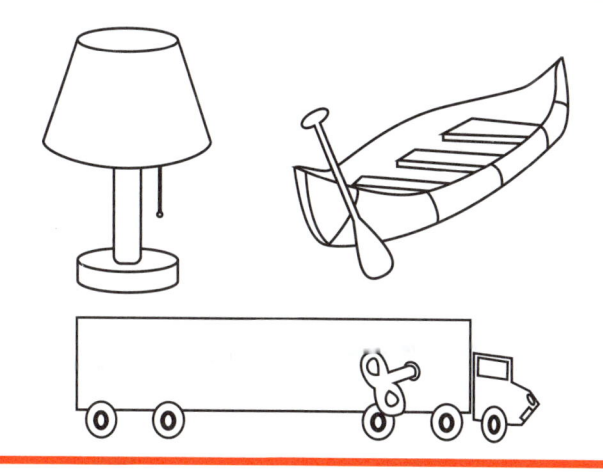

Spectrum Shapes
Kindergarten

Chapter 3, Lesson 13
Identifying Shapes within Pictures

63

NAME _____

Lesson 4.1
DESCRIBING THE ORIENTATION OF OBJECTS

Color the animals that are **above** the cat green. Color the animals that are **below** the cat red. Circle the birds that are **next to** each other.

Spectrum Shapes
Kindergarten
64

Chapter 4, Lesson 1
Describing the Orientation of Objects and Shapes

NAME _____

Lesson 4.1
DESCRIBING THE ORIENTATION OF OBJECTS

Look at the picture. Circle the word or words that tell where the objects are.

The dog is   below   above   next to   the doghouse.

The butterfly is   below   above   next to   the sun.

The bird is   below   above   next to   the butterfly.

The rabbit is   below   above   next to   the other rabbit.

Spectrum Shapes
Kindergarten

Chapter 4, Lesson 1
Describing the Orientation of Objects and Shapes

NAME _____

Lesson 4.2
DESCRIBING THE ORIENTATION OF 2-D SHAPES

Color the triangles that are **below** the bird blue. Color the circle that is **above** the butterflies orange. Color the square that is **next to** the dog green. Color the rectangle that is **near** the frog red.

Spectrum Shapes
Kindergarten
66

Chapter 4, Lesson 2
Describing the Orientation of Objects and Shapes

NAME _____

Lesson 4.2
DESCRIBING THE ORIENTATION OF 2-D SHAPES

Look at the picture. Circle the word or words that tell where the objects are.

The circle is   above   next to   the dog.

The rhombus is   below   above   the dog.

The oval is   below   next to   the butterfly.

The triangles are   above   near   the bird.

Spectrum Shapes
Kindergarten

Chapter 4, Lesson 2
Describing the Orientation of Objects and Shapes

67

Lesson 4.3
DESCRIBING THE ORIENTATION OF 3-D SHAPES

Color the sphere that is **below** the flag orange. Color the rectangular prisms that are **above** the frogs green. Color the cylinder that is **next to** the butterfly red. Color the cubes that are **near** the dog blue.

Spectrum Shapes
Kindergarten

NAME _____

Lesson 4.3
DESCRIBING THE ORIENTATION OF 3-D SHAPES

Look at the picture. Circle the word or words that tell where the objects are.

The sphere is   above   next to   the cat.

The rectangular prism is   below   above   the birds.

The cone is   near   above   the dog.

The cylinder is   below   near   the house.

Spectrum Shapes
Kindergarten

NAME _____

Lesson 5.1
TRACING AND DRAWING 2-D SHAPES

Trace the circle in the sun. Color it yellow. Trace the triangle on the sailboat. Color it blue. Trace the oval. Color it brown.

Spectrum Shapes
Kindergarten

Chapter 5, Lesson 1
Tracing, Drawing, and Composing Shapes

NAME _____

Lesson 5.1
TRACING AND DRAWING 2-D SHAPES

Trace the shape. Draw the shape.

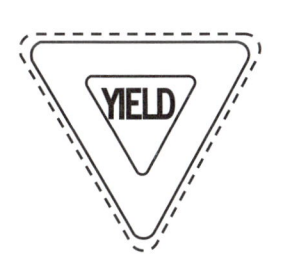

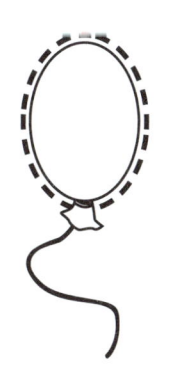

Spectrum Shapes
Kindergarten

Chapter 5, Lesson 1
Tracing, Drawing, and Composing Shapes

71

Lesson 5.1
TRACING AND DRAWING 2-D SHAPES

Trace the shape. Draw the shape.

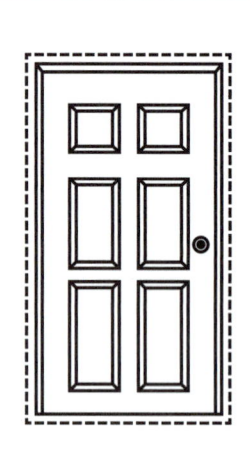

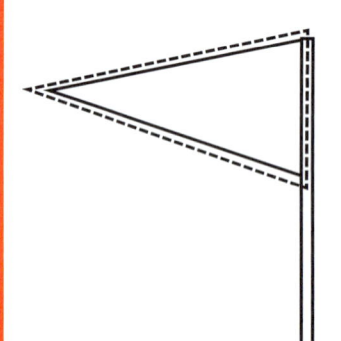

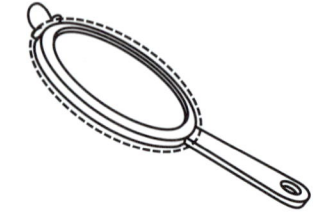

Spectrum Shapes
Kindergarten
72

Chapter 5, Lesson 1
Tracing, Drawing, and Composing Shapes

NAME _____

Lesson 5.2
TRACING AND DRAWING 3-D SHAPES

Trace the shape. Draw the shape.

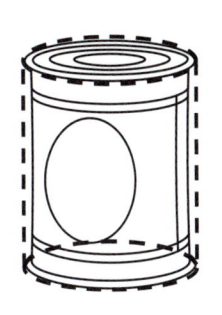

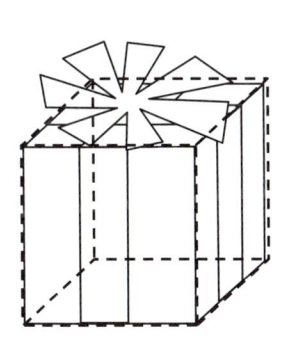

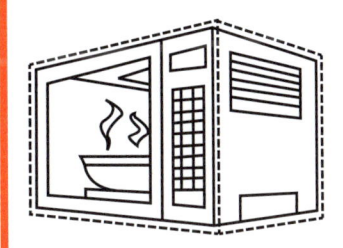

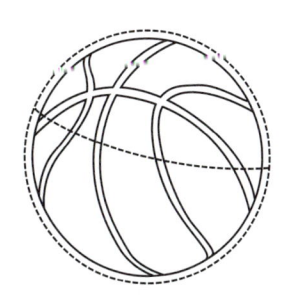

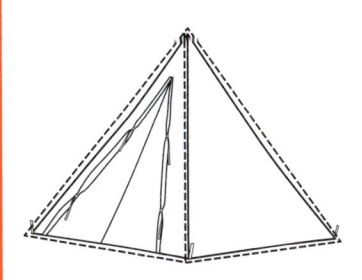

Spectrum Shapes
Kindergarten

Chapter 5, Lesson 2
Tracing, Drawing, and Composing Shapes

73

NAME _____

Lesson 5.2
TRACING AND DRAWING 3-D SHAPES

Trace the shape. Draw the shape.

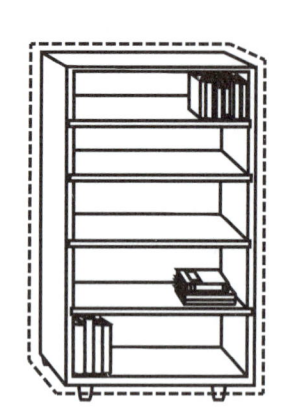

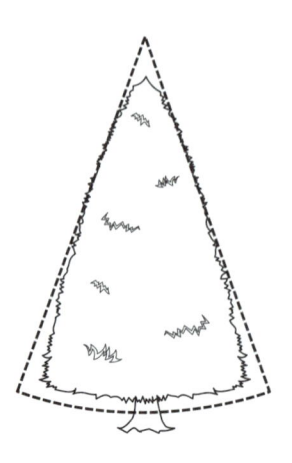

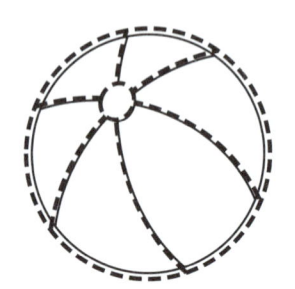

Spectrum Shapes
Kindergarten
74

Chapter 5, Lesson 2
Tracing, Drawing, and Composing Shapes

NAME _____

Lesson 5.3
COMPOSING SIMPLE 2-D SHAPES TO FORM LARGER SHAPES

Put the following shapes together. Trace the shape you get.

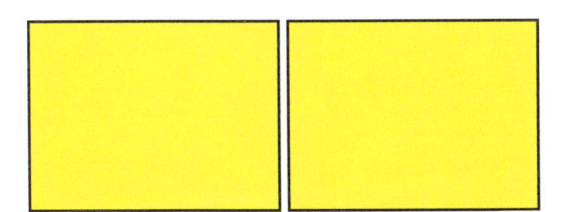

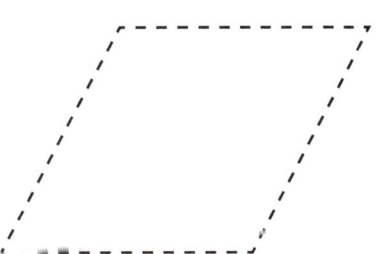

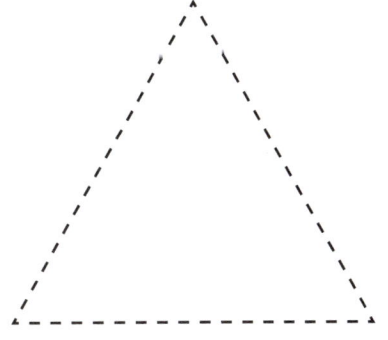

Spectrum Shapes
Kindergarten

Chapter 5, Lesson 3
Tracing, Drawing, and Composing Shapes

75

NAME _____

Lesson 5.3
COMPOSING SIMPLE 2-D SHAPES TO FORM LARGER SHAPES

Put the following shapes together. Trace the shape you get.

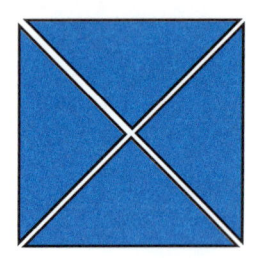

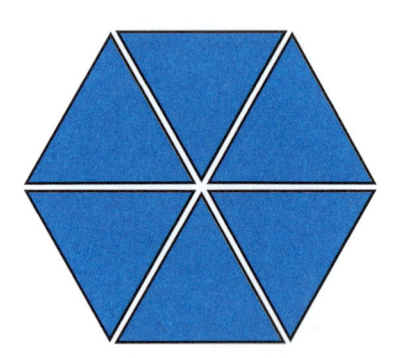

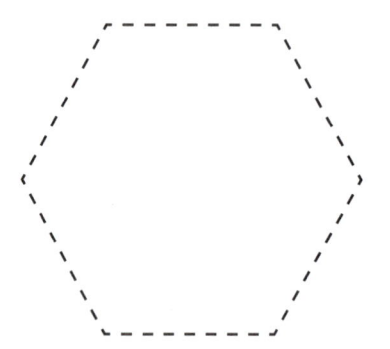

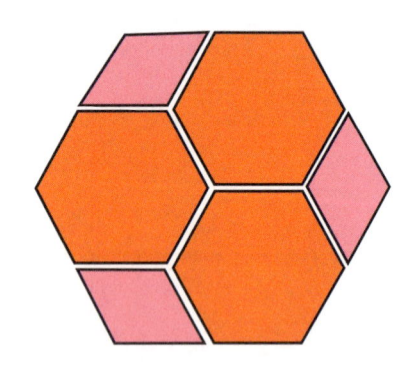

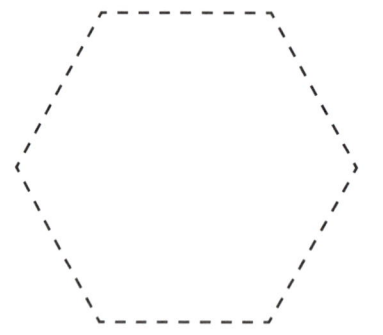

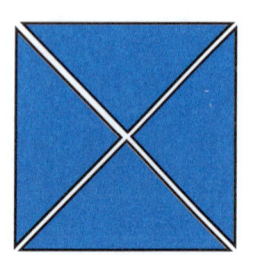

Spectrum Shapes
Kindergarten
76

Chapter 5, Lesson 3
Tracing, Drawing, and Composing Shapes

NAME _____

Lesson 5.3
COMPOSING SIMPLE 2-D SHAPES TO FORM LARGER SHAPES

Put the following shapes together. Trace the shape you get.

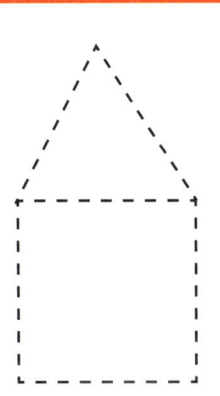

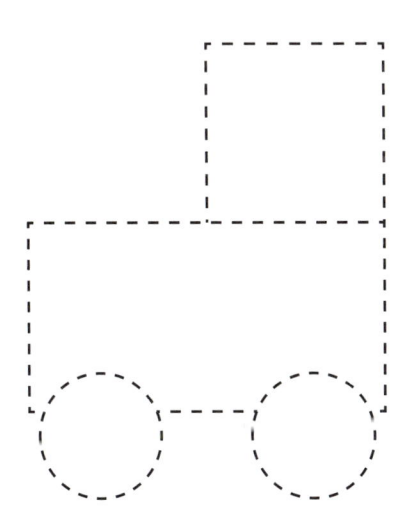

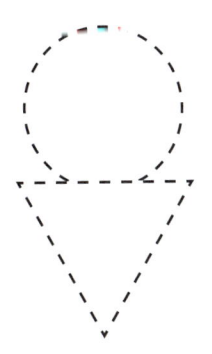

Spectrum Shapes
Kindergarten

Chapter 5, Lesson 3
Tracing, Drawing, and Composing Shapes

77

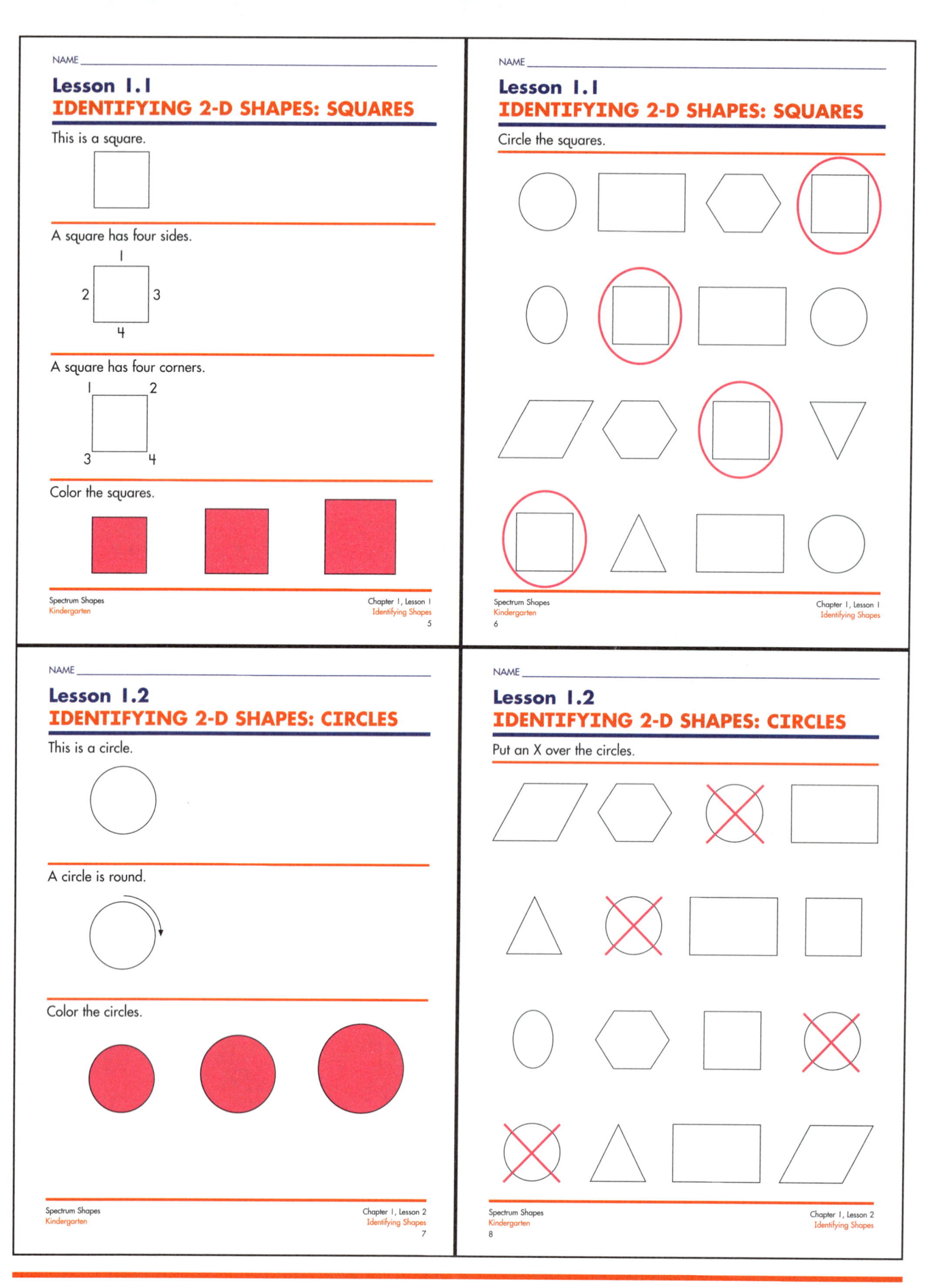

NAME _____

Lesson 1.1
IDENTIFYING 2-D SHAPES: SQUARES

This is a square.

A square has four sides.

A square has four corners.

Color the squares.

Spectrum Shapes
Kindergarten

Chapter 1, Lesson 1
Identifying Shapes
5

NAME _____

Lesson 1.1
IDENTIFYING 2-D SHAPES: SQUARES

Circle the squares.

Spectrum Shapes
Kindergarten
6

Chapter 1, Lesson 1
Identifying Shapes

NAME _____

Lesson 1.2
IDENTIFYING 2-D SHAPES: CIRCLES

This is a circle.

A circle is round.

Color the circles.

Spectrum Shapes
Kindergarten

Chapter 1, Lesson 2
Identifying Shapes
7

NAME _____

Lesson 1.2
IDENTIFYING 2-D SHAPES: CIRCLES

Put an X over the circles.

Spectrum Shapes
Kindergarten
8

Chapter 1, Lesson 2
Identifying Shapes

Spectrum Shapes
Kindergarten

Answer Key

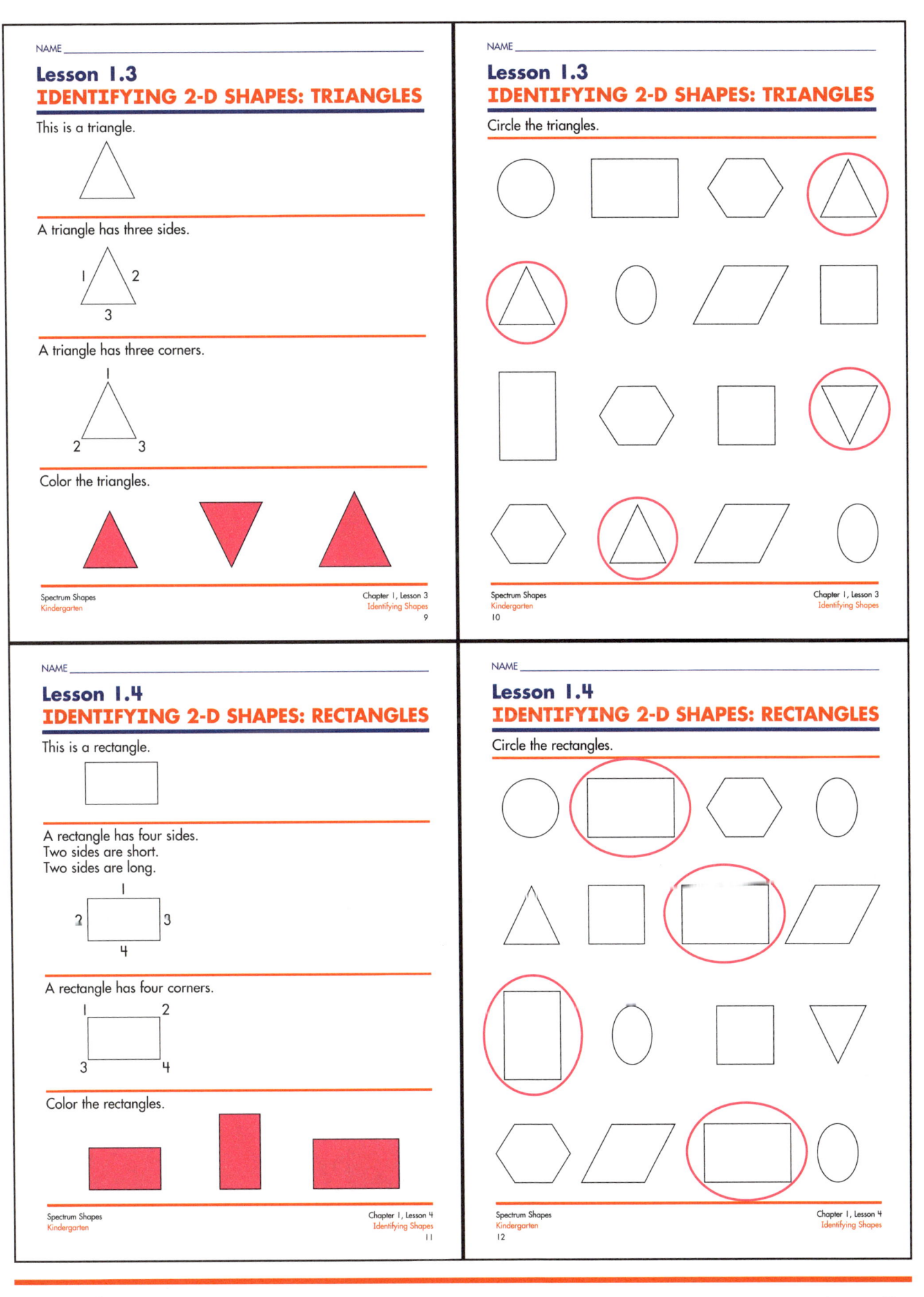

NAME _____

Lesson 1.3
IDENTIFYING 2-D SHAPES: TRIANGLES

This is a triangle.

A triangle has three sides.

A triangle has three corners.

Color the triangles.

Spectrum Shapes
Kindergarten

Chapter 1, Lesson 3
Identifying Shapes
9

NAME _____

Lesson 1.3
IDENTIFYING 2-D SHAPES: TRIANGLES

Circle the triangles.

Spectrum Shapes
Kindergarten

Chapter 1, Lesson 3
Identifying Shapes
10

NAME _____

Lesson 1.4
IDENTIFYING 2-D SHAPES: RECTANGLES

This is a rectangle.

A rectangle has four sides.
Two sides are short.
Two sides are long.

A rectangle has four corners.

Color the rectangles.

Spectrum Shapes
Kindergarten

Chapter 1, Lesson 4
Identifying Shapes
11

NAME _____

Lesson 1.4
IDENTIFYING 2-D SHAPES: RECTANGLES

Circle the rectangles.

Spectrum Shapes
Kindergarten

Chapter 1, Lesson 4
Identifying Shapes
12

Spectrum Shapes
Kindergarten

Answer Key

79

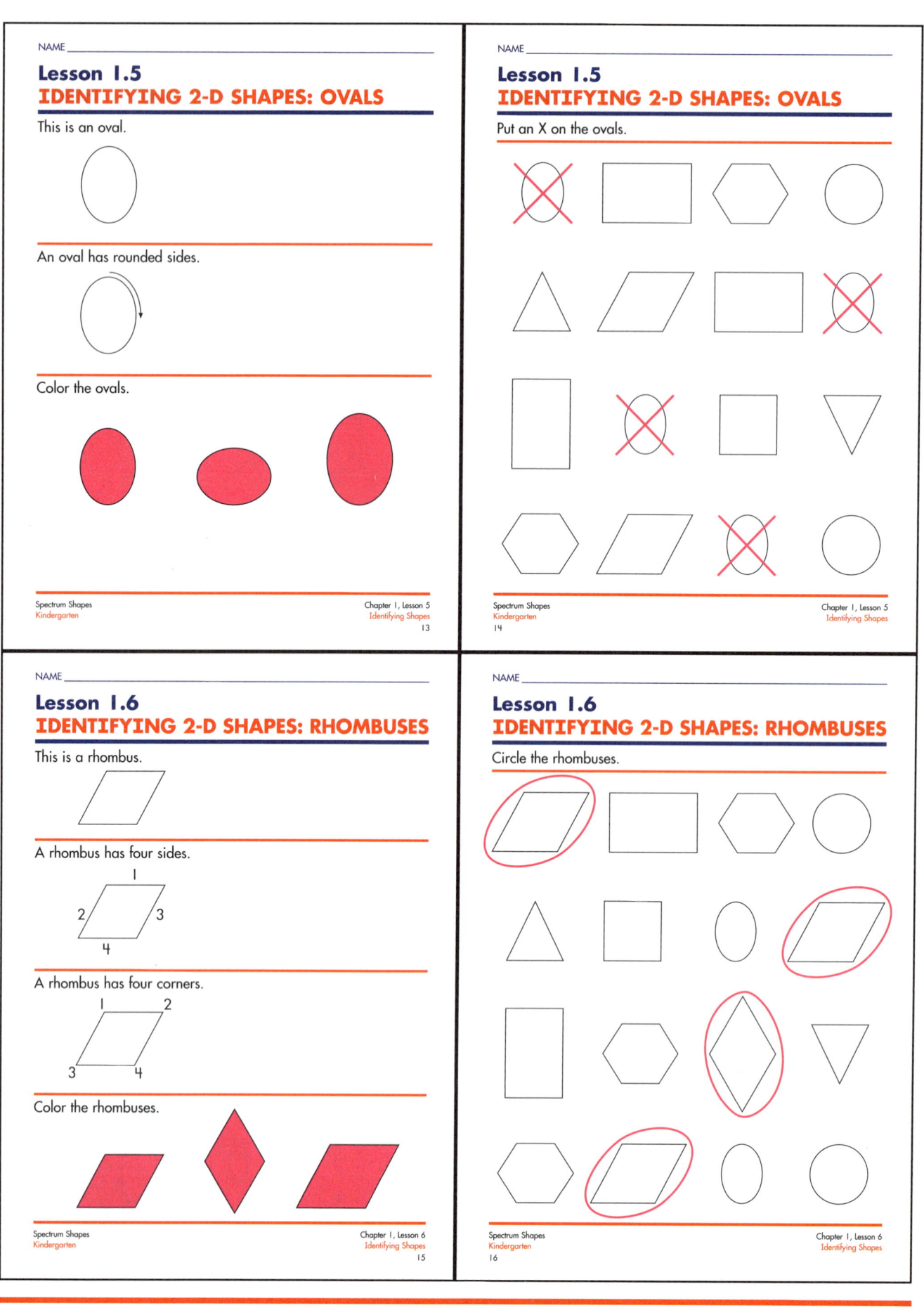

NAME

Lesson 1.5
IDENTIFYING 2-D SHAPES: OVALS

This is an oval.

An oval has rounded sides.

Color the ovals.

Spectrum Shapes
Kindergarten

Chapter 1, Lesson 5
Identifying Shapes
13

NAME

Lesson 1.5
IDENTIFYING 2-D SHAPES: OVALS

Put an X on the ovals.

Spectrum Shapes
Kindergarten
14

Chapter 1, Lesson 5
Identifying Shapes

NAME

Lesson 1.6
IDENTIFYING 2-D SHAPES: RHOMBUSES

This is a rhombus.

A rhombus has four sides.

A rhombus has four corners.

Color the rhombuses.

Spectrum Shapes
Kindergarten

Chapter 1, Lesson 6
Identifying Shapes
15

NAME

Lesson 1.6
IDENTIFYING 2-D SHAPES: RHOMBUSES

Circle the rhombuses.

Spectrum Shapes
Kindergarten
16

Chapter 1, Lesson 6
Identifying Shapes

Spectrum Shapes
Kindergarten

Answer Key

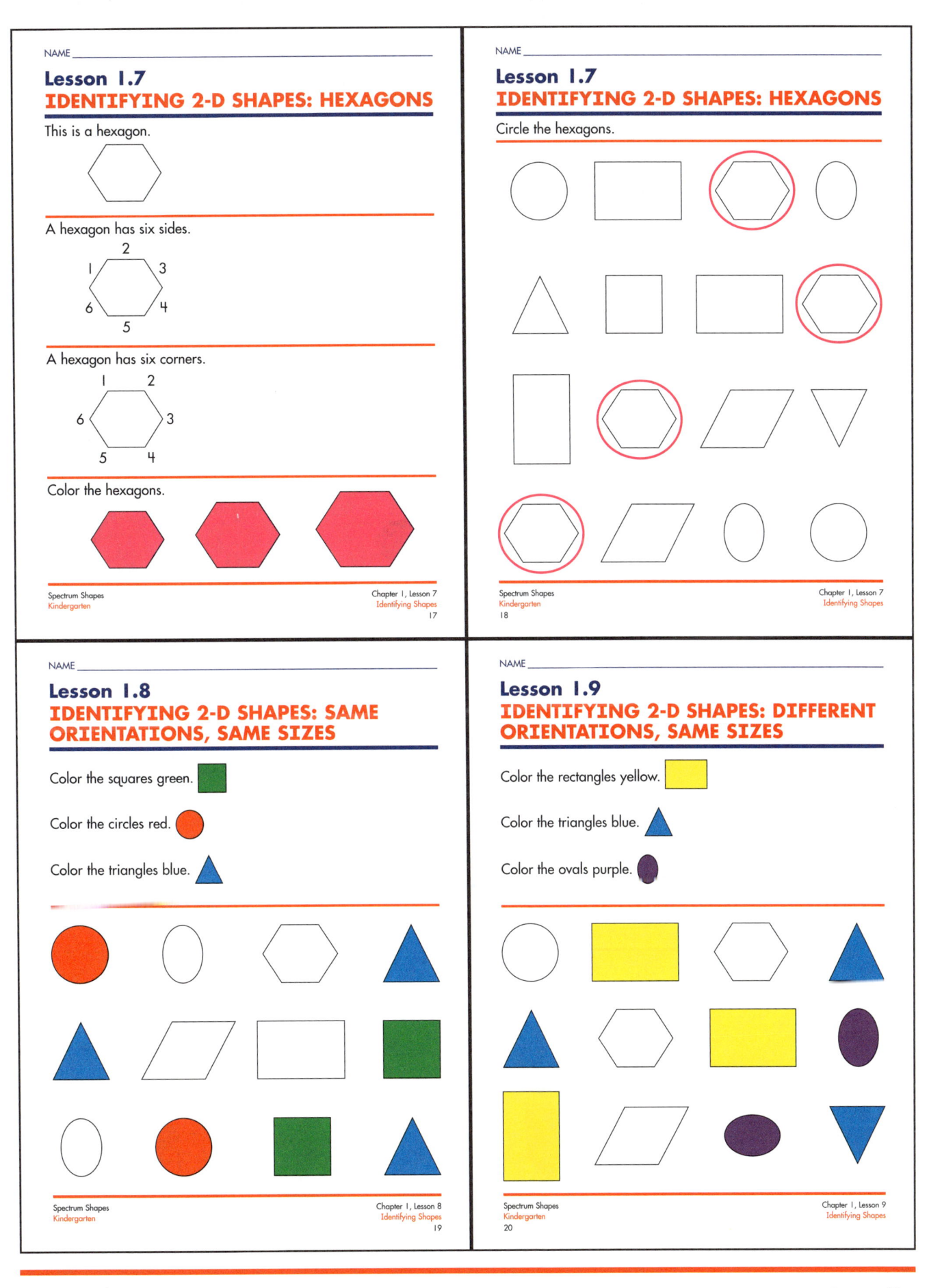

NAME _____

Lesson 1.7
IDENTIFYING 2-D SHAPES: HEXAGONS

This is a hexagon.

A hexagon has six sides.

A hexagon has six corners.

Color the hexagons.

Spectrum Shapes
Kindergarten

Chapter 1, Lesson 7
Identifying Shapes
17

NAME _____

Lesson 1.7
IDENTIFYING 2-D SHAPES: HEXAGONS

Circle the hexagons.

Spectrum Shapes
Kindergarten

Chapter 1, Lesson 7
Identifying Shapes
18

NAME _____

Lesson 1.8
IDENTIFYING 2-D SHAPES: SAME ORIENTATIONS, SAME SIZES

Color the squares green.

Color the circles red.

Color the triangles blue.

Spectrum Shapes
Kindergarten

Chapter 1, Lesson 8
Identifying Shapes
19

NAME _____

Lesson 1.9
IDENTIFYING 2-D SHAPES: DIFFERENT ORIENTATIONS, SAME SIZES

Color the rectangles yellow.

Color the triangles blue.

Color the ovals purple.

Spectrum Shapes
Kindergarten

Chapter 1, Lesson 9
Identifying Shapes
20

Spectrum Shapes
Kindergarten

Answer Key

81

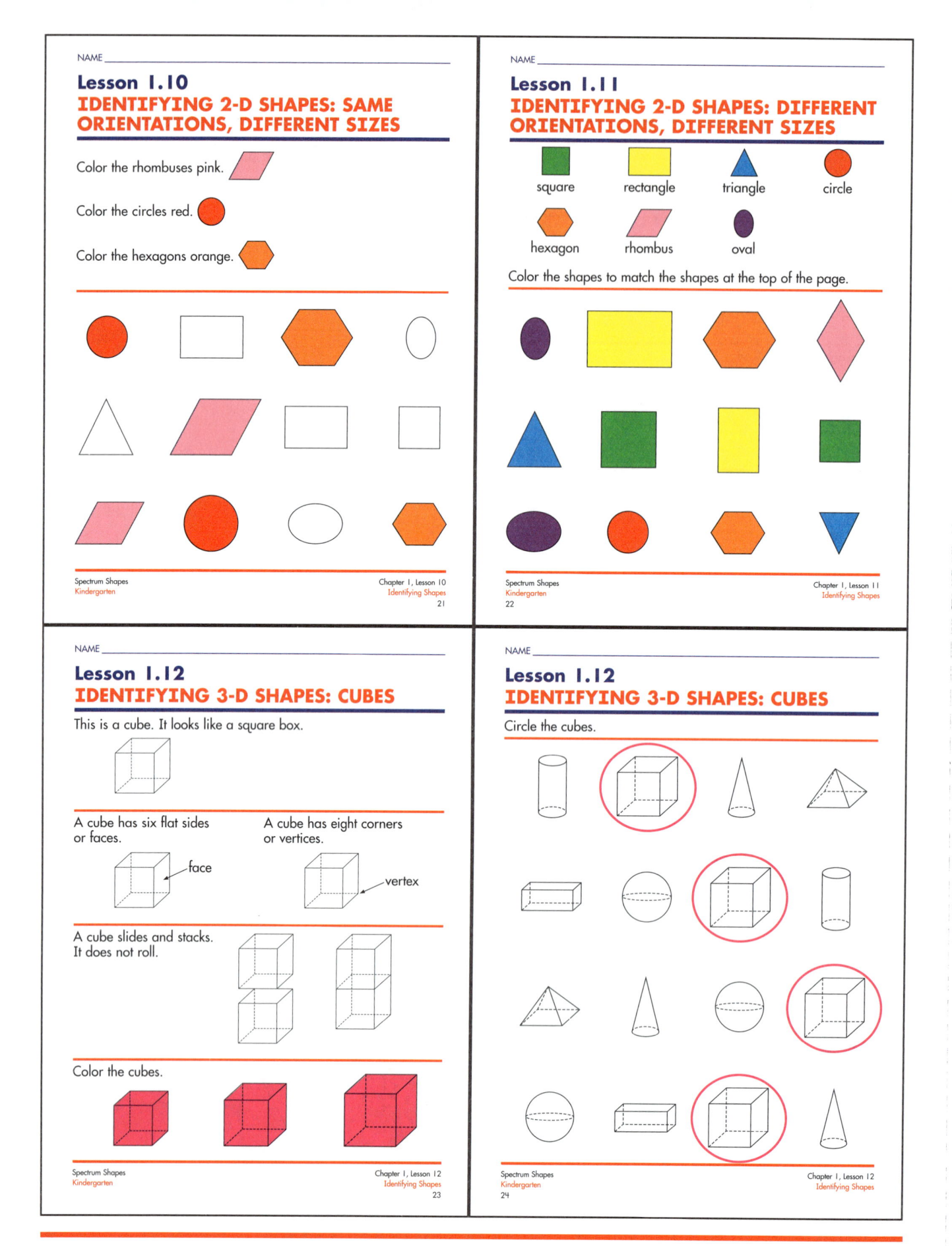

NAME _____

Lesson 1.10
IDENTIFYING 2-D SHAPES: SAME ORIENTATIONS, DIFFERENT SIZES

Color the rhombuses pink.

Color the circles red.

Color the hexagons orange.

Spectrum Shapes
Kindergarten

Chapter 1, Lesson 10
Identifying Shapes
21

NAME _____

Lesson 1.11
IDENTIFYING 2-D SHAPES: DIFFERENT ORIENTATIONS, DIFFERENT SIZES

square   rectangle   triangle   circle

hexagon   rhombus   oval

Color the shapes to match the shapes at the top of the page.

Spectrum Shapes
Kindergarten

Chapter 1, Lesson 11
Identifying Shapes
22

NAME _____

Lesson 1.12
IDENTIFYING 3-D SHAPES: CUBES

This is a cube. It looks like a square box.

A cube has six flat sides or faces. — face

A cube has eight corners or vertices. — vertex

A cube slides and stacks. It does not roll.

Color the cubes.

Spectrum Shapes
Kindergarten

Chapter 1, Lesson 12
Identifying Shapes
23

NAME _____

Lesson 1.12
IDENTIFYING 3-D SHAPES: CUBES

Circle the cubes.

Spectrum Shapes
Kindergarten

Chapter 1, Lesson 12
Identifying Shapes
24

Spectrum Shapes
Kindergarten

Answer Key

82

NAME _____

Lesson 1.13
IDENTIFYING 3-D SHAPES: SPHERES

This is a sphere. It looks like a ball.

A sphere has curved sides.

A sphere rolls. It does not stack.

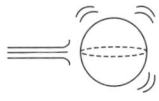

Color the spheres.

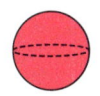

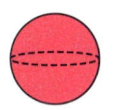

Spectrum Shapes
Kindergarten

Chapter 1, Lesson 13
Identifying Shapes
25

NAME _____

Lesson 1.13
IDENTIFYING 3-D SHAPES: SPHERES

Put an X on the spheres.

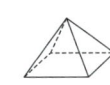

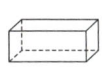

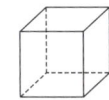

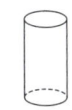

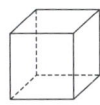

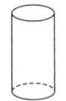

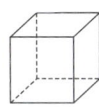

Spectrum Shapes
Kindergarten

Chapter 1, Lesson 13
Identifying Shapes
26

NAME _____

Lesson 1.14
IDENTIFYING 3-D SHAPES: PYRAMIDS

This is a pyramid.

A pyramid has four flat sides or faces.
These faces are shaped like triangles.

A pyramid also has a face on the bottom.
This face is shaped like a square.

Color the pyramids.

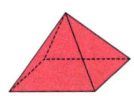

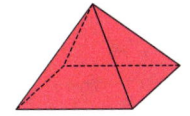

Spectrum Shapes
Kindergarten

Chapter 1, Lesson 14
Identifying Shapes
27

NAME _____

Lesson 1.14
IDENTIFYING 3-D SHAPES: PYRAMIDS

Circle the pyramids.

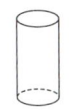

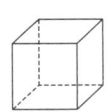

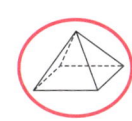

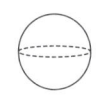

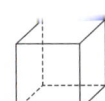

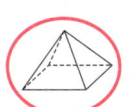

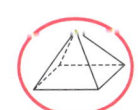

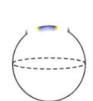

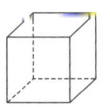

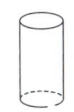

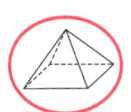

Spectrum Shapes
Kindergarten

Chapter 1, Lesson 14
Identifying Shapes
28

Spectrum Shapes
Kindergarten

Answer Key

83

NAME _____

Lesson 1.15
IDENTIFYING 3-D SHAPES: RECTANGULAR PRISMS

This is a rectangular prism.

A rectangular prism has six flat sides or faces. ← face

A rectangular prism has eight corners or vertices. ← vertex

A rectangular prism slides and stacks. It does not roll.

Color the rectangular prisms.

Spectrum Shapes
Kindergarten

Chapter 1, Lesson 15
Identifying Shapes
29

NAME _____

Lesson 1.15
IDENTIFYING 3-D SHAPES: RECTANGULAR PRISMS

Circle the rectangular prisms.

Spectrum Shapes
Kindergarten

Chapter 1, Lesson 15
Identifying Shapes
30

NAME _____

Lesson 1.16
IDENTIFYING 3-D SHAPES: CONES

This is a cone. It looks like an ice cream cone.

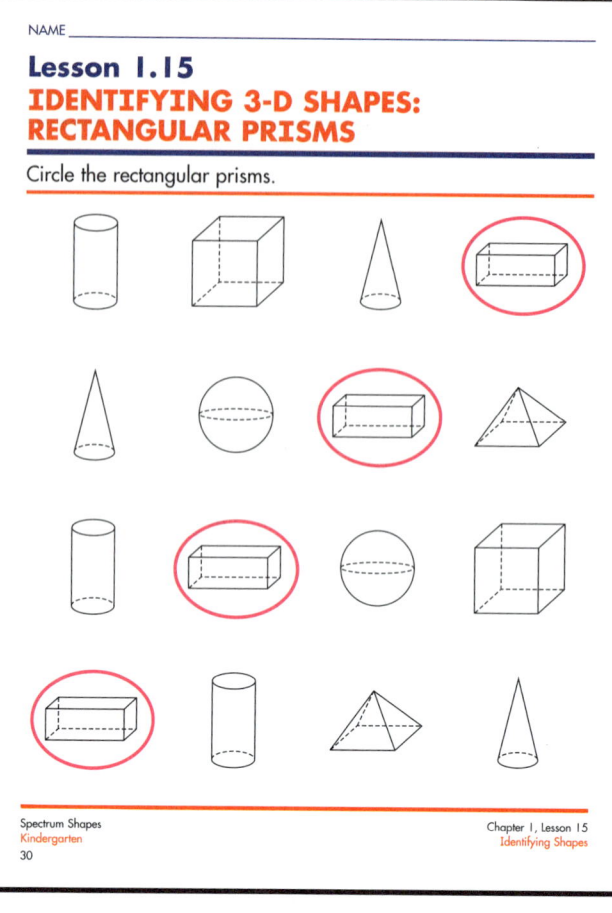

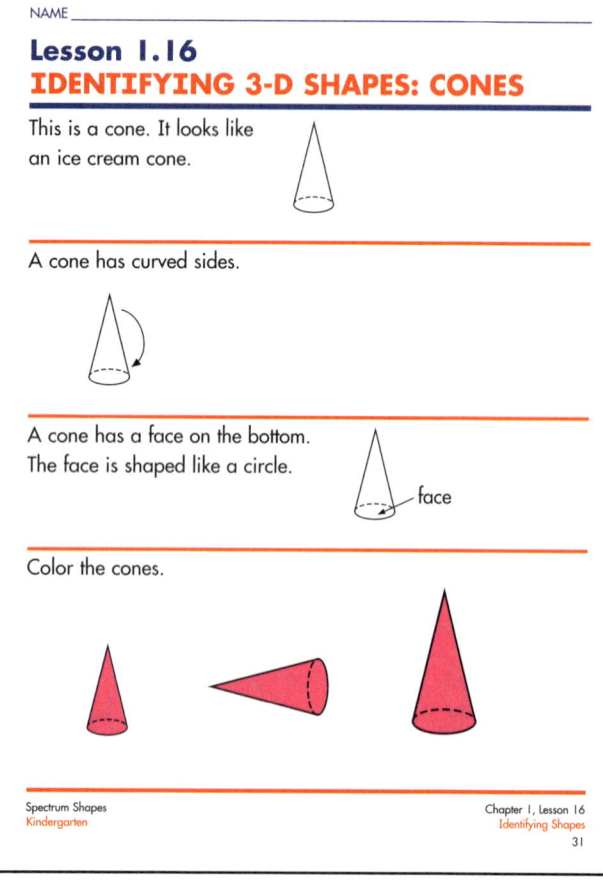

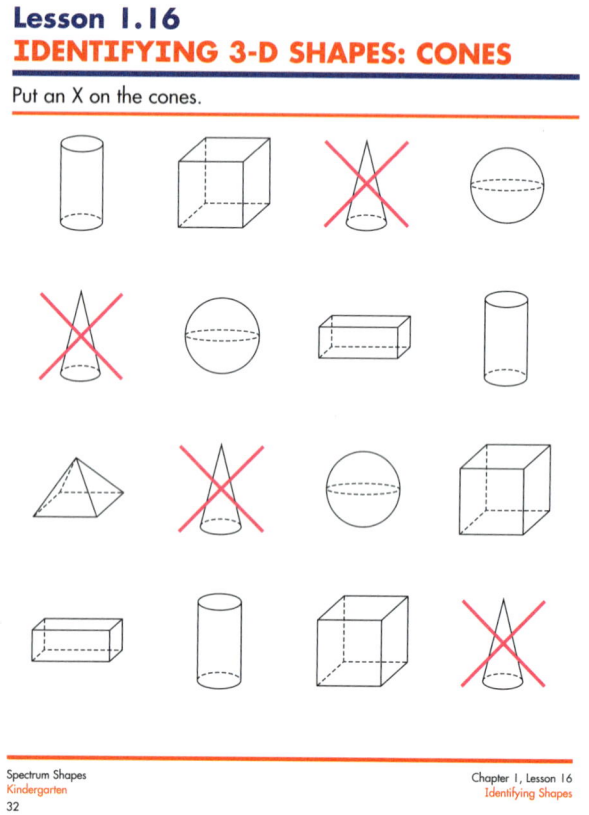

A cone has curved sides.

A cone has a face on the bottom. The face is shaped like a circle. ← face

Color the cones.

Spectrum Shapes
Kindergarten

Chapter 1, Lesson 16
Identifying Shapes
31

NAME _____

Lesson 1.16
IDENTIFYING 3-D SHAPES: CONES

Put an X on the cones.

Spectrum Shapes
Kindergarten

Chapter 1, Lesson 16
Identifying Shapes
32

Spectrum Shapes
Kindergarten

Answer Key

84

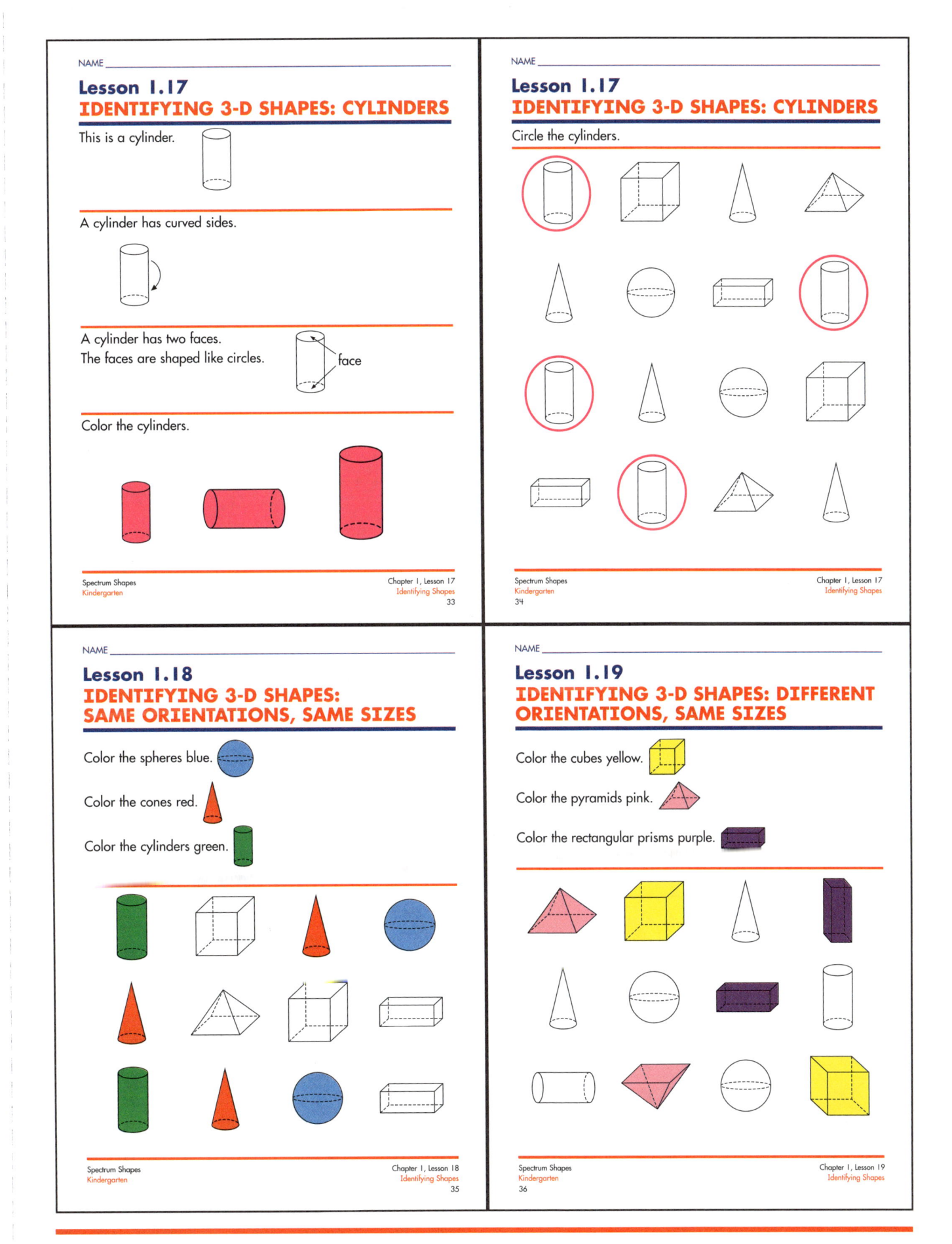

NAME

Lesson 1.17
IDENTIFYING 3-D SHAPES: CYLINDERS

This is a cylinder.

A cylinder has curved sides.

A cylinder has two faces.
The faces are shaped like circles.

Color the cylinders.

Spectrum Shapes
Kindergarten

Chapter 1, Lesson 17
Identifying Shapes
33

NAME

Lesson 1.17
IDENTIFYING 3-D SHAPES: CYLINDERS

Circle the cylinders.

Spectrum Shapes
Kindergarten
34

Chapter 1, Lesson 17
Identifying Shapes

NAME

Lesson 1.18
IDENTIFYING 3-D SHAPES: SAME ORIENTATIONS, SAME SIZES

Color the spheres blue.

Color the cones red.

Color the cylinders green.

Spectrum Shapes
Kindergarten

Chapter 1, Lesson 18
Identifying Shapes
35

NAME

Lesson 1.19
IDENTIFYING 3-D SHAPES: DIFFERENT ORIENTATIONS, SAME SIZES

Color the cubes yellow.

Color the pyramids pink.

Color the rectangular prisms purple.

Spectrum Shapes
Kindergarten
36

Chapter 1, Lesson 19
Identifying Shapes

Spectrum Shapes
Kindergarten

Answer Key

85

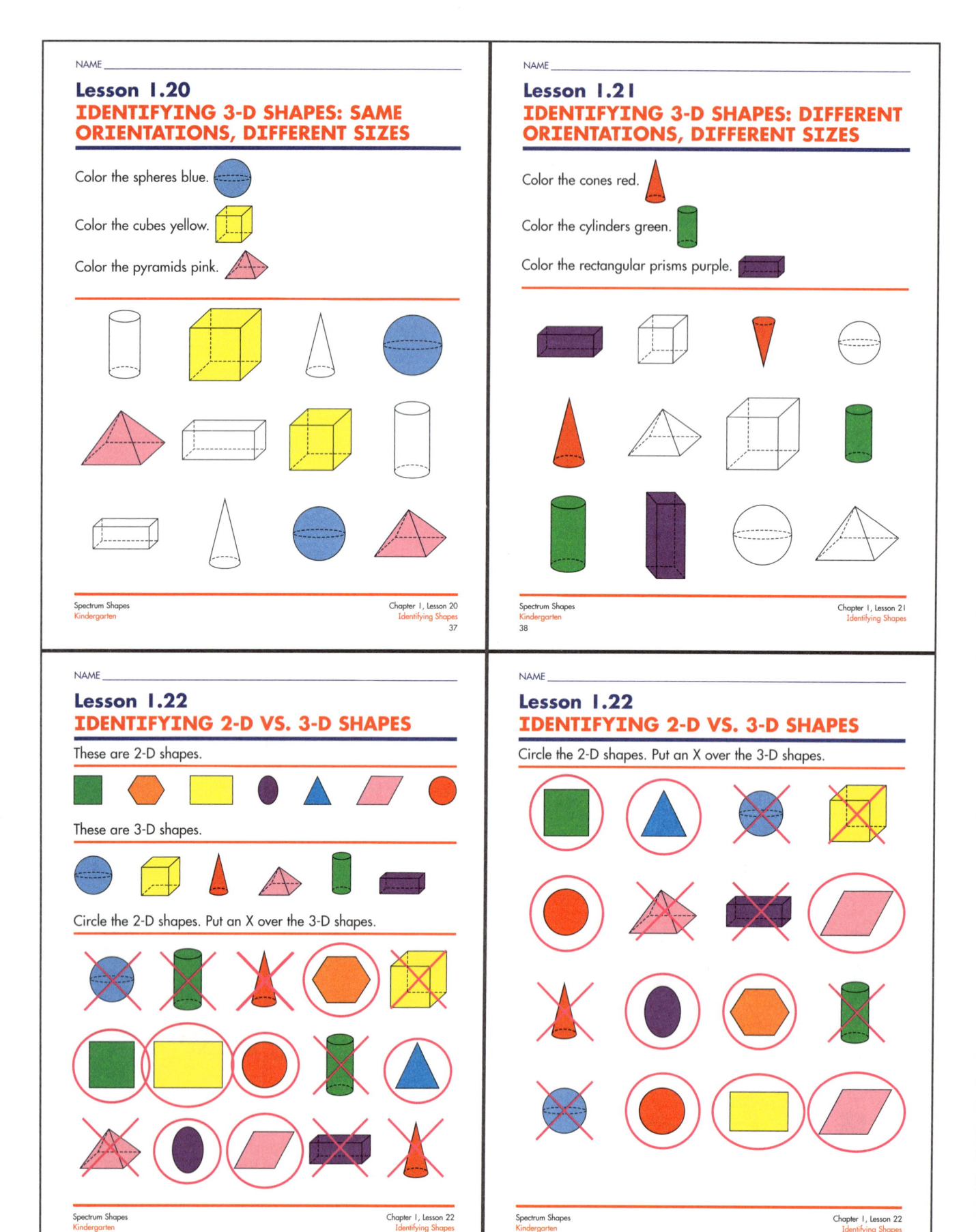

NAME _____

Lesson 1.20
IDENTIFYING 3-D SHAPES: SAME ORIENTATIONS, DIFFERENT SIZES

Color the spheres blue.

Color the cubes yellow.

Color the pyramids pink.

Spectrum Shapes
Kindergarten

Chapter 1, Lesson 20
Identifying Shapes
37

NAME _____

Lesson 1.21
IDENTIFYING 3-D SHAPES: DIFFERENT ORIENTATIONS, DIFFERENT SIZES

Color the cones red.

Color the cylinders green.

Color the rectangular prisms purple.

Spectrum Shapes
Kindergarten

Chapter 1, Lesson 21
Identifying Shapes
38

NAME _____

Lesson 1.22
IDENTIFYING 2-D VS. 3-D SHAPES

These are 2-D shapes.

These are 3-D shapes.

Circle the 2-D shapes. Put an X over the 3-D shapes.

Spectrum Shapes
Kindergarten

Chapter 1, Lesson 22
Identifying Shapes
39

NAME _____

Lesson 1.22
IDENTIFYING 2-D VS. 3-D SHAPES

Circle the 2-D shapes. Put an X over the 3-D shapes.

Spectrum Shapes
Kindergarten

Chapter 1, Lesson 22
Identifying Shapes
40

Spectrum Shapes
Kindergarten

Answer Key

86

NAME _____

Lesson 1.22
IDENTIFYING 2-D VS. 3-D SHAPES

Color the 2-D shapes red. Color the 3-D shapes blue.

Spectrum Shapes
Kindergarten

Chapter 1, Lesson 22
Identifying Shapes
41

NAME _____

Lesson 1.22
IDENTIFYING 2-D VS. 3-D SHAPES

Circle the 2-D shapes. Put an X over the 3-D shapes.

Spectrum Shapes
Kindergarten

Chapter 1, Lesson 22
Identifying Shapes
42

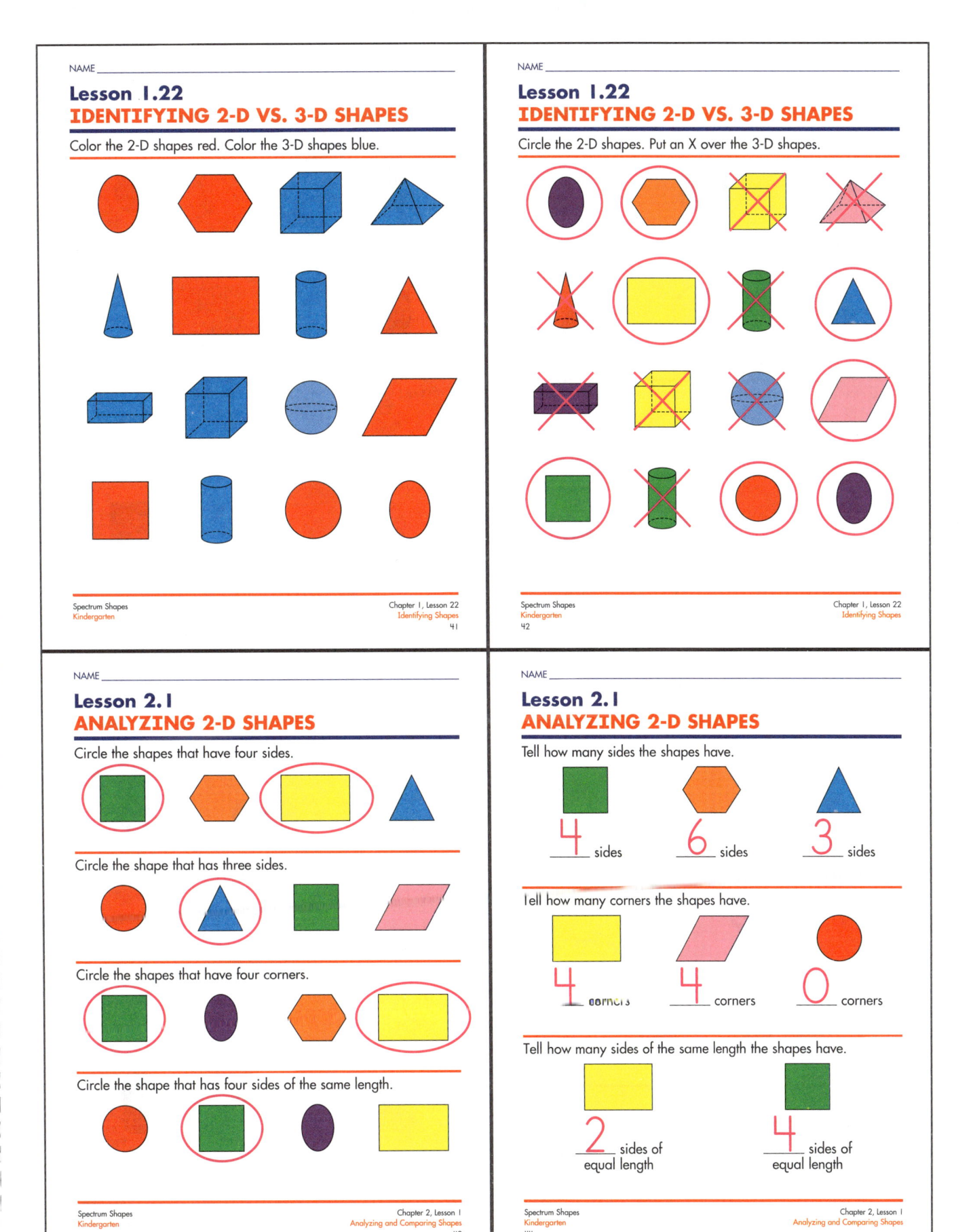

NAME _____

Lesson 2.1
ANALYZING 2-D SHAPES

Circle the shapes that have four sides.

Circle the shape that has three sides.

Circle the shapes that have four corners.

Circle the shape that has four sides of the same length.

Spectrum Shapes
Kindergarten

Chapter 2, Lesson 1
Analyzing and Comparing Shapes
43

NAME _____

Lesson 2.1
ANALYZING 2-D SHAPES

Tell how many sides the shapes have.

__4__ sides   __6__ sides   __3__ sides

Tell how many corners the shapes have.

__4__ corners   __4__ corners   __0__ corners

Tell how many sides of the same length the shapes have.

__2__ sides of equal length   __4__ sides of equal length

Spectrum Shapes
Kindergarten

Chapter 2, Lesson 1
Analyzing and Comparing Shapes
44

Spectrum Shapes
Kindergarten

Answer Key

87

Lesson 2.2
COMPARING 2-D SHAPES

Circle the shapes that have four sides.

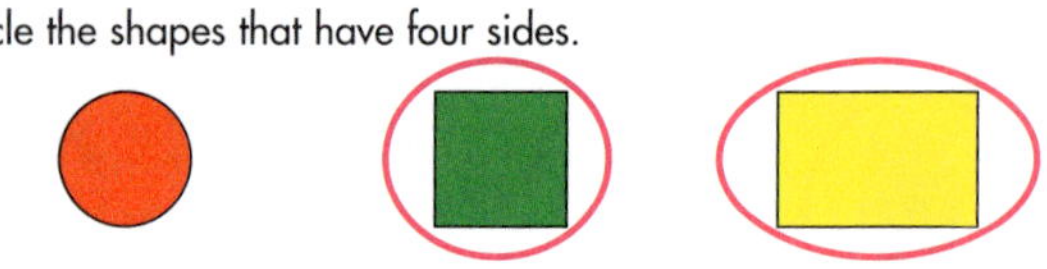

Circle the shapes that are curved.

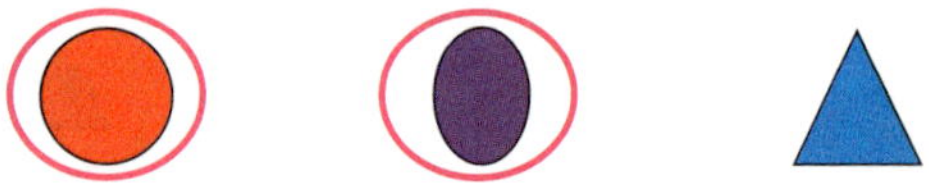

Circle the shapes that have straight sides.

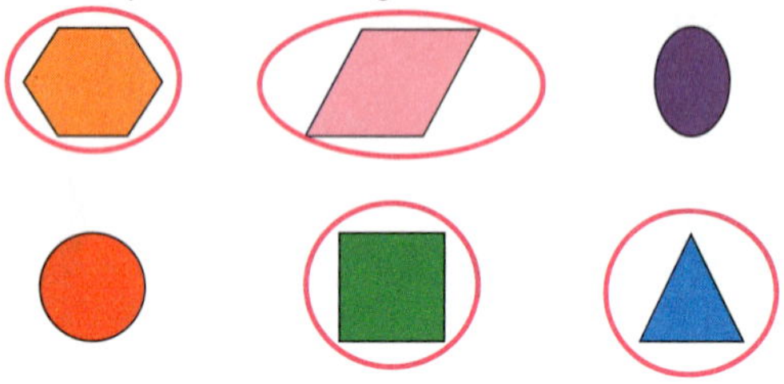

Lesson 2.2
COMPARING 2-D SHAPES

Cross out the shape that is not curved.

Cross out the shape that does not have four sides.

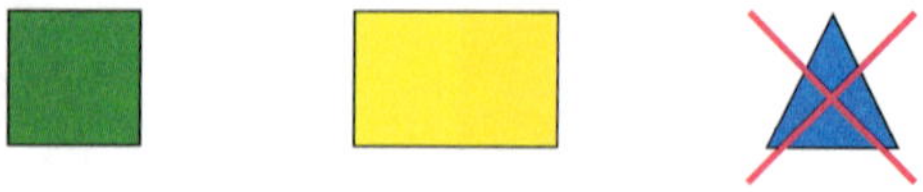

Cross out the shapes that do not have straight sides.

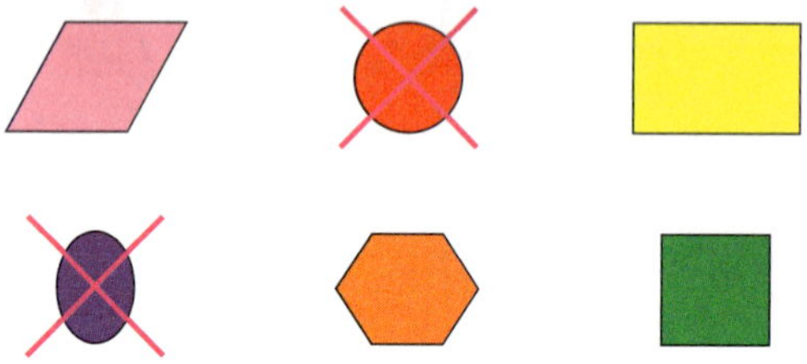

Lesson 2.3
ANALYZING 3-D SHAPES

Circle the shapes that have six faces.

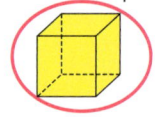

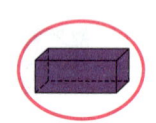

Circle the shape that has no faces.

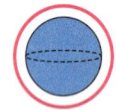

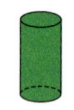

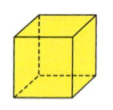

Circle the shapes that roll.

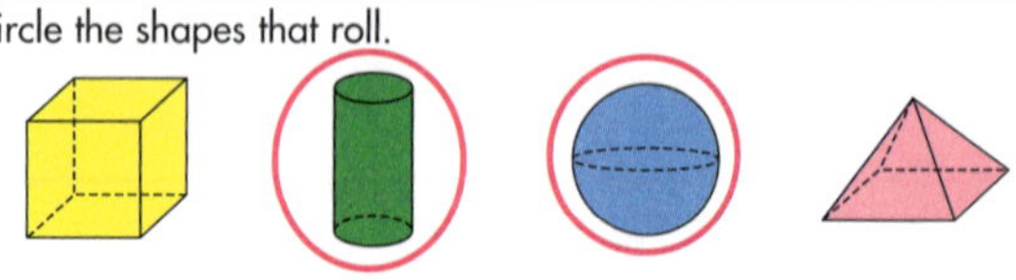

Circle the shapes that stack.

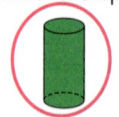

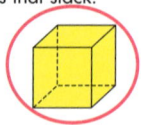

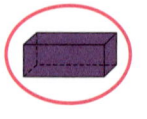

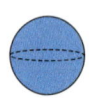

Lesson 2.3
ANALYZING 3-D SHAPES

Tell how many faces the shapes have.

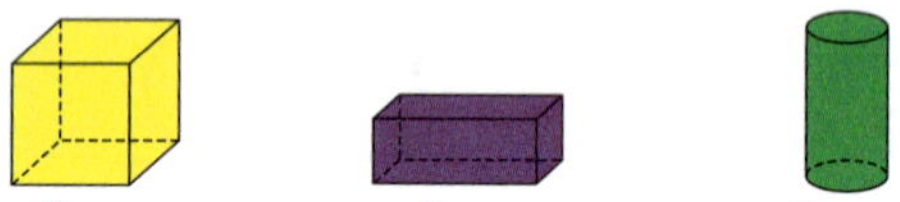

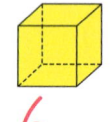

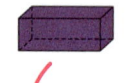

___6___ faces   ___6___ faces   ___2___ faces

Tell how many corners the shapes have.

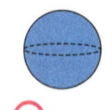

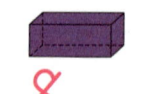

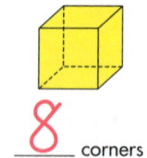

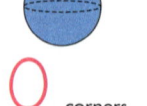

___0___ corners   ___8___ corners   ___8___ corners

Draw the shape of the faces.

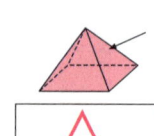

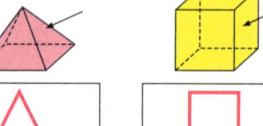

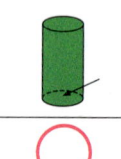

Spectrum Shapes
Kindergarten

Answer Key

NAME

Lesson 2.4
COMPARING 3-D SHAPES

Circle the shapes that have square faces.

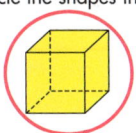

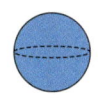

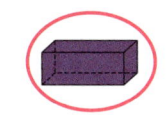

Circle the shapes that have circles for faces.

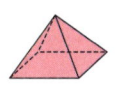

Circle the shapes that both stack and roll.

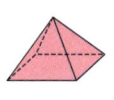

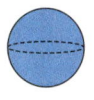

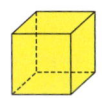

Spectrum Shapes
Kindergarten

Chapter 2, Lesson 4
Analyzing and Comparing Shapes
49

NAME

Lesson 2.4
COMPARING 3-D SHAPES

Cross out the shape that does not stack.

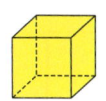

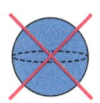

Cross out the shape that does not have curved sides.

Cross out the shapes that do not have a square face.

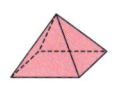

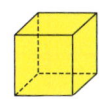

Spectrum Shapes
Kindergarten
50

Chapter 2, Lesson 4
Analyzing and Comparing Shapes

NAME

Lesson 3.1
IDENTIFYING 2-D SHAPES WITHIN PICTURES: SQUARES

Color the square shapes green.

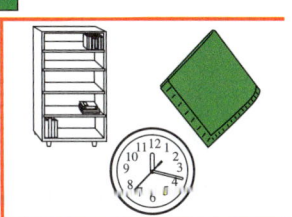

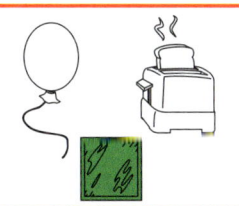

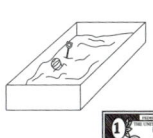

Spectrum Shapes
Kindergarten

Chapter 3, Lesson 1
Identifying Shapes within Pictures
51

NAME

Lesson 3.2
IDENTIFYING 2-D SHAPES WITHIN PICTURES: CIRCLES

Color the circle shapes red.

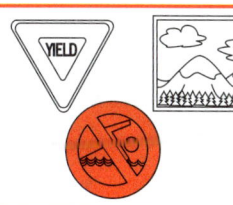

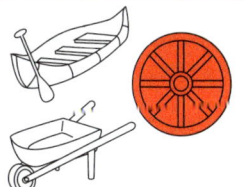

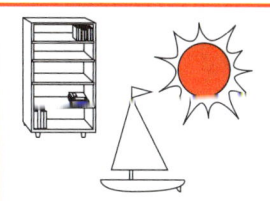

Spectrum Shapes
Kindergarten
52

Chapter 3, Lesson 2
Identifying Shapes within Pictures

Spectrum Shapes
Kindergarten

Answer Key

89

NAME _____

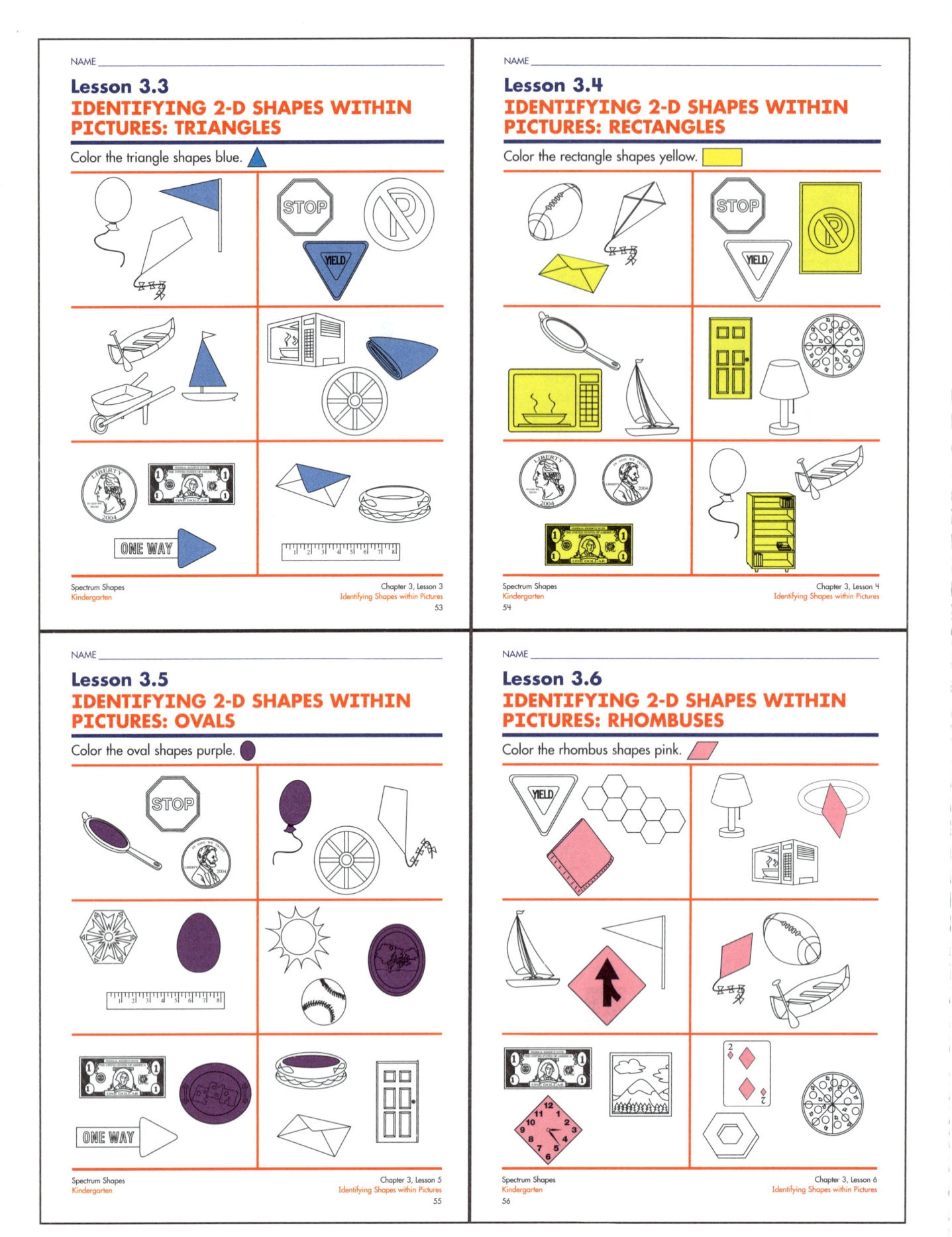

Lesson 3.3
IDENTIFYING 2-D SHAPES WITHIN PICTURES: TRIANGLES

Color the triangle shapes blue.

Spectrum Shapes
Kindergarten

Chapter 3, Lesson 3
Identifying Shapes within Pictures
53

NAME _____

Lesson 3.4
IDENTIFYING 2-D SHAPES WITHIN PICTURES: RECTANGLES

Color the rectangle shapes yellow.

Spectrum Shapes
Kindergarten

Chapter 3, Lesson 4
Identifying Shapes within Pictures
54

NAME _____

Lesson 3.5
IDENTIFYING 2-D SHAPES WITHIN PICTURES: OVALS

Color the oval shapes purple.

Spectrum Shapes
Kindergarten

Chapter 3, Lesson 5
Identifying Shapes within Pictures
55

NAME _____

Lesson 3.6
IDENTIFYING 2-D SHAPES WITHIN PICTURES: RHOMBUSES

Color the rhombus shapes pink.

Spectrum Shapes
Kindergarten

Chapter 3, Lesson 6
Identifying Shapes within Pictures
56

Spectrum Shapes
Kindergarten

Answer Key

90

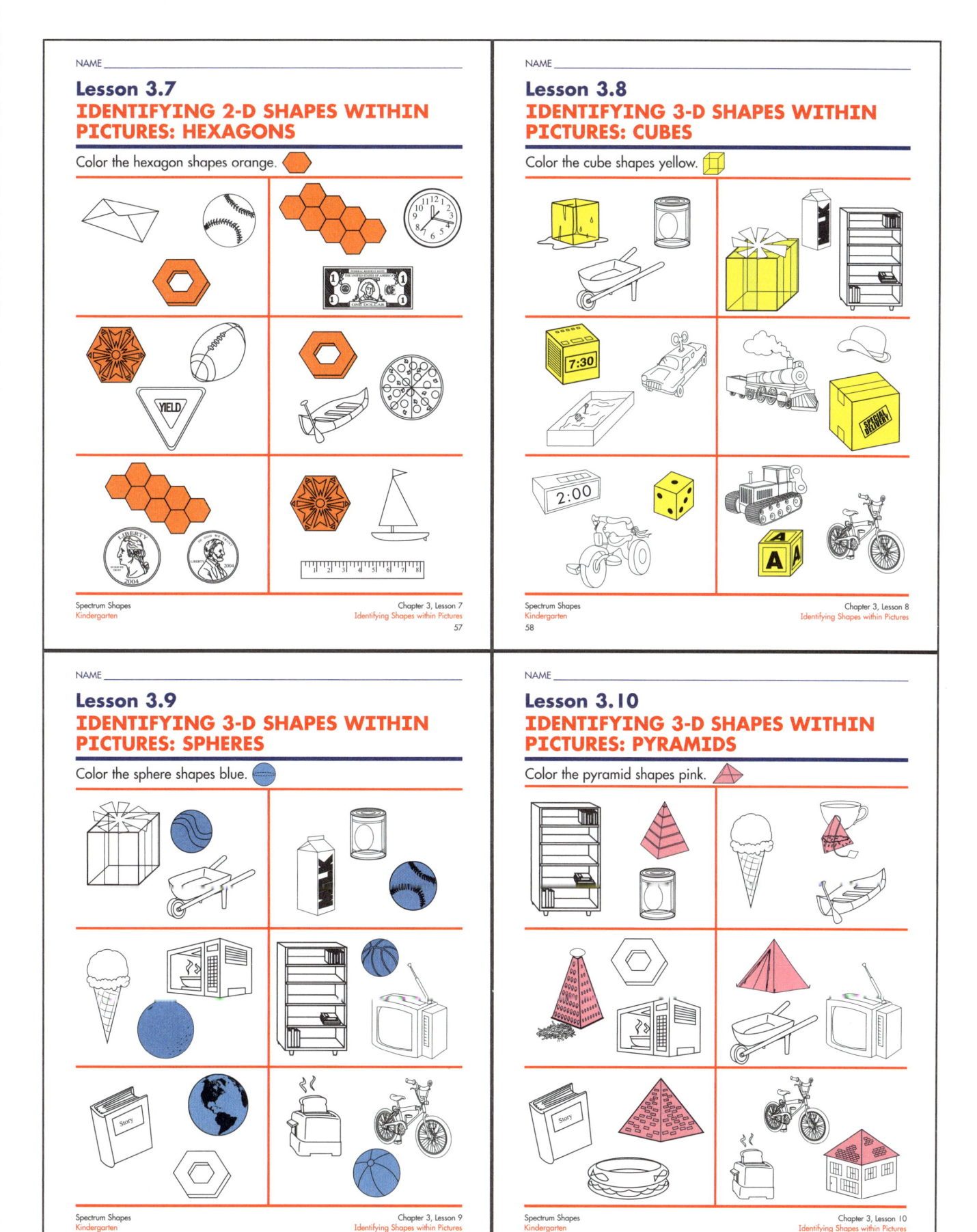

NAME _____

Lesson 3.7
IDENTIFYING 2-D SHAPES WITHIN PICTURES: HEXAGONS

Color the hexagon shapes orange.

Spectrum Shapes
Kindergarten

Chapter 3, Lesson 7
Identifying Shapes within Pictures
57

NAME _____

Lesson 3.8
IDENTIFYING 3-D SHAPES WITHIN PICTURES: CUBES

Color the cube shapes yellow.

Spectrum Shapes
Kindergarten

Chapter 3, Lesson 8
Identifying Shapes within Pictures
58

NAME _____

Lesson 3.9
IDENTIFYING 3-D SHAPES WITHIN PICTURES: SPHERES

Color the sphere shapes blue.

Spectrum Shapes
Kindergarten

Chapter 3, Lesson 9
Identifying Shapes within Pictures
59

NAME _____

Lesson 3.10
IDENTIFYING 3-D SHAPES WITHIN PICTURES: PYRAMIDS

Color the pyramid shapes pink.

Spectrum Shapes
Kindergarten

Chapter 3, Lesson 10
Identifying Shapes within Pictures
60

Spectrum Shapes
Kindergarten

Answer Key

91

NAME _____

Lesson 3.11
IDENTIFYING 3-D SHAPES WITHIN PICTURES: RECTANGULAR PRISMS

Color the rectangular prism shapes purple.

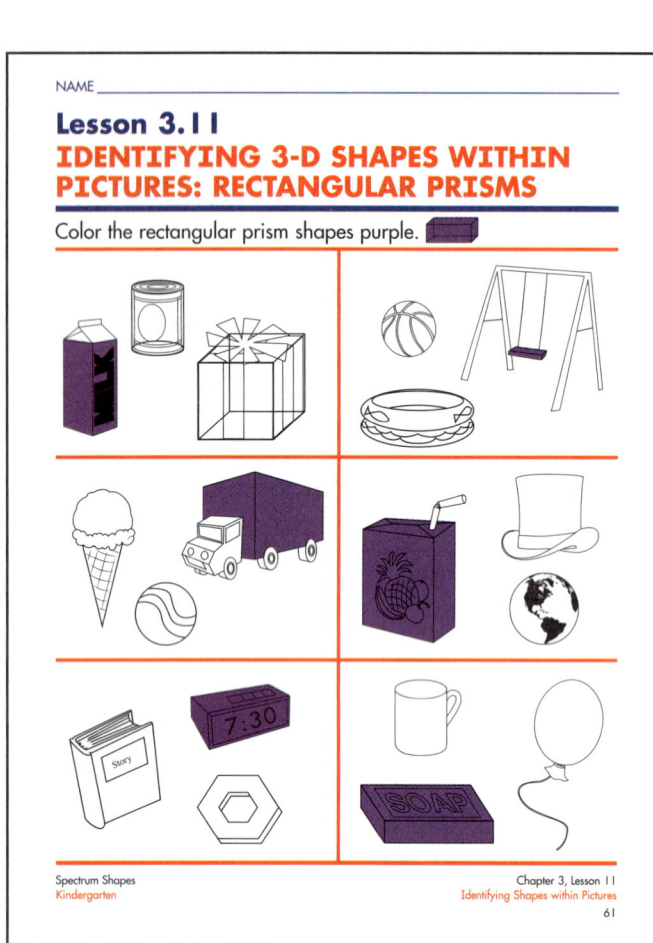

Spectrum Shapes
Kindergarten

Chapter 3, Lesson 11
Identifying Shapes within Pictures
61

NAME _____

Lesson 3.12
IDENTIFYING 3-D SHAPES WITHIN PICTURES: CONES

Color the cone shapes red.

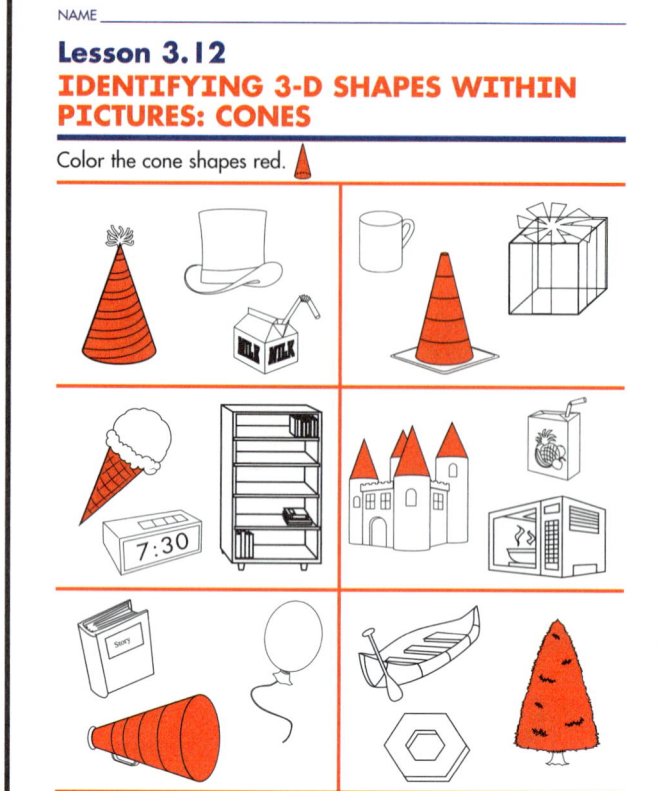

Spectrum Shapes
Kindergarten

Chapter 3, Lesson 12
Identifying Shapes within Pictures
62

NAME _____

Lesson 3.13
IDENTIFYING 3-D SHAPES WITHIN PICTURES: CYLINDERS

Color the cylinder shapes green.

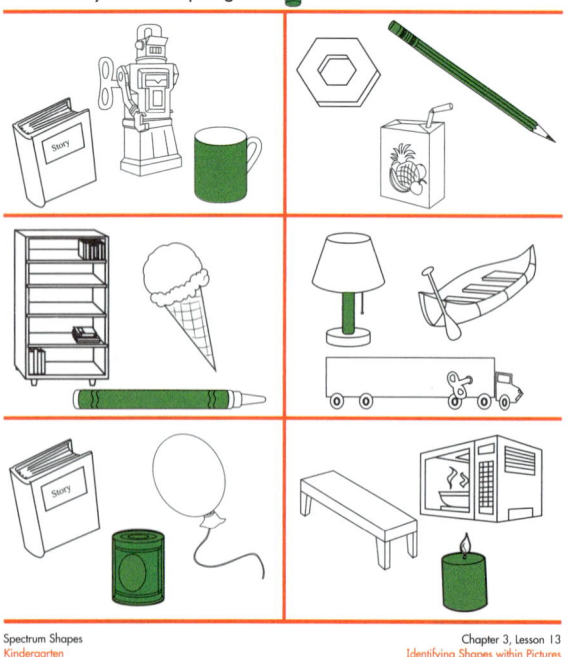

Spectrum Shapes
Kindergarten

Chapter 3, Lesson 13
Identifying Shapes within Pictures
63

NAME _____

Lesson 4.1
DESCRIBING THE ORIENTATION OF OBJECTS

Color the animals that are **above** the cat green. Color the animals that are **below** the cat red. Circle the birds that are **next to** each other.

Spectrum Shapes
Kindergarten

Chapter 4, Lesson 1
Describing the Orientation of Objects and Shapes
64

Spectrum Shapes
Kindergarten
92

Answer Key

NAME _____

Lesson 4.1
DESCRIBING THE ORIENTATION OF OBJECTS

Look at the picture. Circle the word or words that tell where the objects are.

The dog is   below   (above)   next to   the doghouse.
The butterfly is   below   above   (next to)   the sun.
The bird is   (below)   above   next to   the butterfly.
The rabbit is   below   above   (next to)   the other rabbit.

Spectrum Shapes
Kindergarten

NAME _____

Lesson 4.2
DESCRIBING THE ORIENTATION OF 2-D SHAPES

Color the triangles that are **below** the bird blue. Color the circle that is **above** the butterflies orange. Color the square that is **next to** the dog green. Color the rectangle that is **near** the frog red.

Spectrum Shapes
Kindergarten

NAME _____

Lesson 4.2
DESCRIBING THE ORIENTATION OF 2-D SHAPES

Look at the picture. Circle the word or words that tell where the objects are.

The circle is   (above)   next to   the dog.
The rhombus is   (below)   above   the dog.
The oval is   below   (next to)   the butterfly.
The triangles are   above   (near)   the bird.

Spectrum Shapes
Kindergarten

NAME _____

Lesson 4.3
DESCRIBING THE ORIENTATION OF 3-D SHAPES

Color the sphere that is **below** the flag orange. Color the rectangular prisms that are **above** the frogs green. Color the cylinder that is **next to** the butterfly red. Color the cubes that are **near** the dog blue.

Spectrum Shapes
Kindergarten

Spectrum Shapes
Kindergarten

Answer Key

93

NAME _____

Lesson 4.3
DESCRIBING THE ORIENTATION OF 3-D SHAPES

Look at the picture. Circle the word or words that tell where the objects are.

The sphere is   above   (next to)   the cat.
The rectangular prism is   (below)   above   the birds.
The cone is   near   (above)   the dog.
The cylinder is   below   (near)   the house.

Spectrum Shapes
Kindergarten

Chapter 4, Lesson 3
Describing the Orientation of Objects and Shapes
69

NAME _____

Lesson 5.1
TRACING AND DRAWING 2-D SHAPES

Trace the circle in the sun. Color it yellow. Trace the triangle on the sailboat. Color it blue. Trace the oval. Color it brown.

Spectrum Shapes
Kindergarten

Chapter 5, Lesson 1
Tracing, Drawing, and Composing Shapes
70

NAME _____

Lesson 5.1
TRACING AND DRAWING 2-D SHAPES

Trace the shape. Draw the shape.

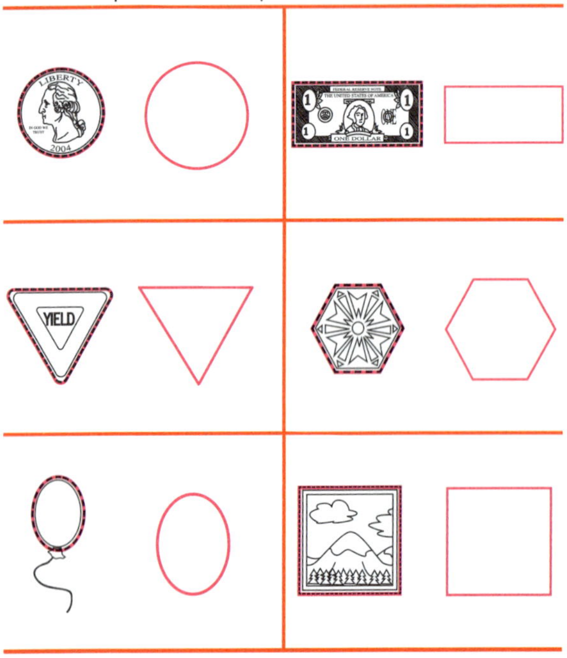

Spectrum Shapes
Kindergarten

Chapter 5, Lesson 1
Tracing, Drawing, and Composing Shapes
71

NAME _____

Lesson 5.1
TRACING AND DRAWING 2-D SHAPES

Trace the shape. Draw the shape.

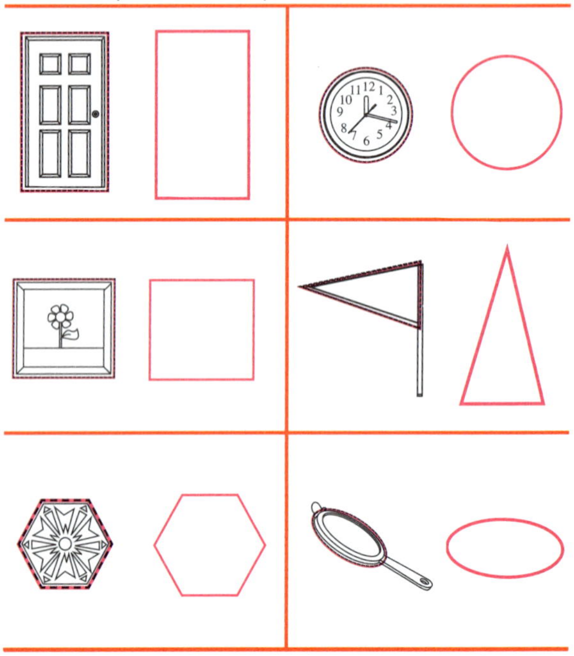

Spectrum Shapes
Kindergarten

Chapter 5, Lesson 1
Tracing, Drawing, and Composing Shapes
72

Spectrum Shapes
Kindergarten
94

Answer Key

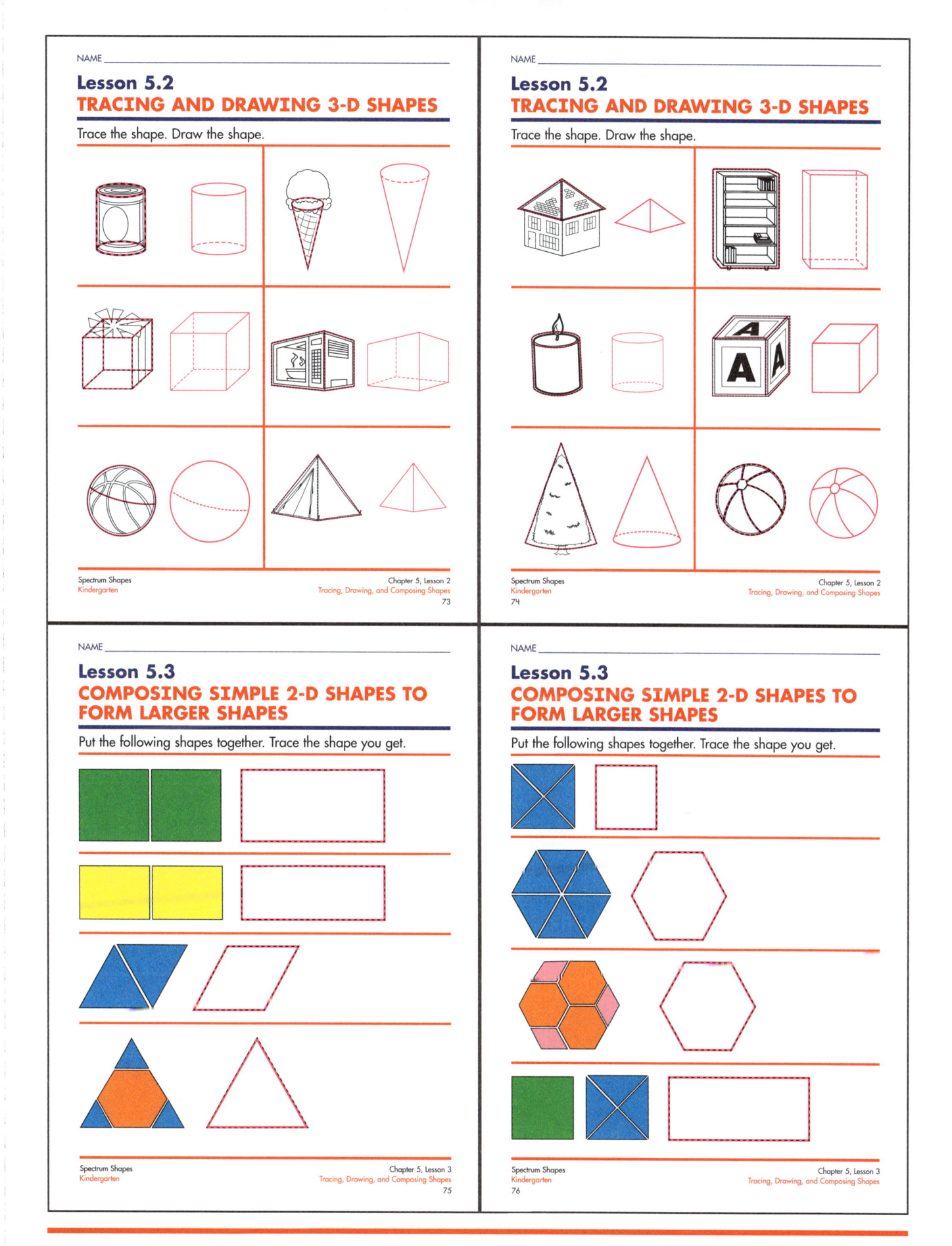

NAME

Lesson 5.2
TRACING AND DRAWING 3-D SHAPES

Trace the shape. Draw the shape.

Spectrum Shapes
Kindergarten

Chapter 5, Lesson 2
Tracing, Drawing, and Composing Shapes
73

NAME

Lesson 5.2
TRACING AND DRAWING 3-D SHAPES

Trace the shape. Draw the shape.

Spectrum Shapes
Kindergarten

Chapter 5, Lesson 2
Tracing, Drawing, and Composing Shapes
74

NAME

Lesson 5.3
COMPOSING SIMPLE 2-D SHAPES TO FORM LARGER SHAPES

Put the following shapes together. Trace the shape you get.

Spectrum Shapes
Kindergarten

Chapter 5, Lesson 3
Tracing, Drawing, and Composing Shapes
75

NAME

Lesson 5.3
COMPOSING SIMPLE 2-D SHAPES TO FORM LARGER SHAPES

Put the following shapes together. Trace the shape you get.

Spectrum Shapes
Kindergarten

Chapter 5, Lesson 3
Tracing, Drawing, and Composing Shapes
76

Spectrum Shapes
Kindergarten

Answer Key

95

NAME

Lesson 5.3
COMPOSING SIMPLE 2-D SHAPES TO FORM LARGER SHAPES

Put the following shapes together. Trace the shape you get.

Spectrum Shapes
Kindergarten

Chapter 5, Lesson 3
Tracing, Drawing, and Composing Shapes
77

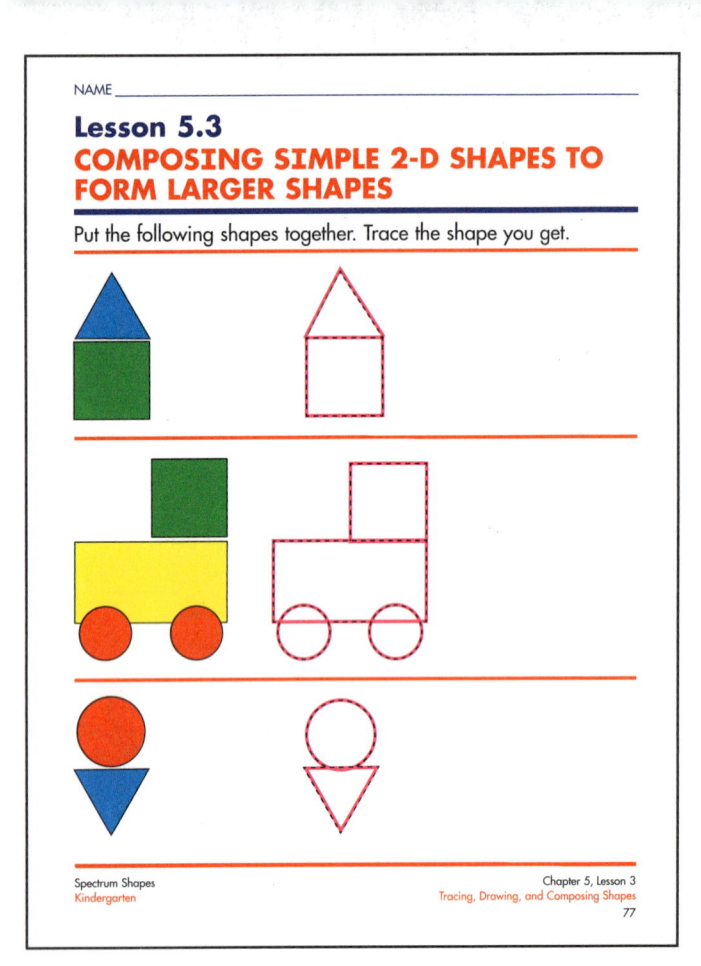